Richard Jefferies

Restless human hearts

Richard Jefferies

Restless human hearts

ISBN/EAN: 9783744736169

Printed in Europe, USA, Canada, Australia, Japan

Cover: Foto ©Andreas Hilbeck / pixelio.de

More available books at **www.hansebooks.com**

RESTLESS HUMAN HEARTS.

A Novel.

BY

RICHARD JEFFERIES,

AUTHOR OF 'THE SCARLET SHAWL.'

IN THREE VOLUMES.

VOL. I.

LONDON:
TINSLEY BROTHERS, 8 CATHERINE ST. STRAND.
1875.

RESTLESS HUMAN HEARTS.

CHAPTER I.

On strictly rational principles, Hotspur's ridicule of Glendower's high pretensions is sufficiently correct. 'When I was born,' says the magician and mystic,

> ' The front of heaven was full of fiery shapes.'

To which Hotspur, as pertly as a chambermaid, replies, that it was equally so when the kittens of that year came into existence. The advent of a comet may herald the birth of a cat as much as a Cæsar.

To trace any connection between the por-

B

tent in the sky and the earthly event is irrational and absurd. All this is true enough. But yet the lives of some among us do seem in some peculiar way to correspond with the singularities of nature. The coincidence may be merely accidental—but there it is; and a highly-wrought mind, dwelling upon its own aspirations and analysing its emotions, can hardly help feeling its individuality increased when it recognises these parallel circumstances. In their turn, the circumstances react upon the creature, and tend to produce a frame of mind strangely susceptible to mystic influences. It is thus that Renan, in the famous *Vie de Jésus*, accounts for what he describes as the delusions which occupied the mind of that central figure of history. The scenery of Judea—the romantic hills and plains, the seas and woods—heightened an originally poetical temperament, till a tension of the mind was produced in which it became capable of the most extraordinary efforts.

So many of us now dwell in an atmosphere of smoke and a scenery composed of brick walls, that the existence of persons whose whole being vibrates to the subtle and invisible touch of Nature seems almost incredible, and certainly absurd. Yet such men and women are living at this day; and well for the world and society that they do, for they act as air-holes, as breathing places, through the thick crust of artificialism, which weighs us down more and more year by year, and they let in a little of the divine light and ether, to purify the air and vivify the corrupting mass.

Laugh at them as much as ye please, ye habitués of the glass-and-iron, veneer-and-varnish palaces of our time. ' Eat, drink, and be merry,' as they did of old. In modern phrase, 'Smoke, swill, and sneer.' The temple in Leicester-square is the fit and appropriate dwelling for your god. Latterly the approach has been cleared to do it honour: fountains play, flowers grow, statues stand in symbolical attitudes. In the warm autumn atmosphere the Moorish pinnacles rise up, glittering with the evening sunlight, and the gaudy temple glows as its hour comes nigh.

The dead brown leaves, driven by the wind, penetrate even into stony London, and rustle along the pavement and whirl round in eddies at the corners of the street. They are a voice from the woods, an echo from the forgotten land, messengers from Nature, abiding still in her solitudes, warning wilful and blinded men to return ere it be too late. But listen! The music rises, and the great hall is full of delicious sound. The dancers gather on the stage, and the flow of wit and joy and song begins. Go not to the Brocken—Walpurgis Night comes here every evening. The lights are gleaming in magic circles; the beauteous witches are floating round. Let us go in and be happy. Who would care to stray on the shore alone, watching the sunset over the waves and the advent of the first lone silvery star? They would sneer at us. The odour of gas is better than the fresh and briny breeze. Yet the delight in the artificial is not altogether an acquired taste only. How is it, else, that the freshest and purest heart, beating warmly with the generous blood of youth, longs so eagerly for the feverish excitements of society?

'O, isn't it lovely?' cried impetuous Heloise, settling herself upon her seat in a box in the Haymarket, with a radiant smile upon her face. 'But only think, we are late: the first act is begun.'

'Late!' said Louis, sneering as usual. 'It it ten minutes past eight. What fools we must look! There are only two other boxes occupied, and one of those is full of children. The *cognoscenti* will take us for paid applauders; we come so regularly and so soon.'

'Paid applauders! What do you mean?' asked Heloise, never taking her gaze from the stage.

'The success of a piece, my dear, depends upon the number of boxes taken. When the pit people see the boxes full, they say, "O, this must be good — see, *they* are here!" Therefore the manager sends his superfluous actors into the empty boxes. Have I made it clear to you, my dear child?'

But she was absorbed in the drama, and

did not hear his mocking tone. Louis looked at her fixedly for a moment or two, with his mouth a little open—much as a country rustic might stare at a real live duke ; then he drew back somewhat, and, turning away from the stage, began to read the latest edition of his evening paper. He soon tired of that.

This is the age of verbiage. Everything must be so long and spun out. No matter how clever a novel may be, the publishers will not issue it unless it will extend to six or seven hundred printed pages. The same plot and characters condensed into two hundred and fifty would be interesting, even exciting; but drawn out to this melancholy length, it is simply a bore. It is equally so with scientific books, and works that pretend to some amount of solidity. They must all be bulky, or they may remain in the author's desk, unpublished and unread. Now it takes a whole life to invent, and afterwards elaborate and bring to a shapely form, one single new idea. Take, for instance, any of the great authors. Look at Goethe. It is all very well to talk about *Wilhelm Meister* and the *Auto-biography*, and the rest—books which our grandfathers read—but the one idea by which Goethe became a living personality to the multitude was his creation of *Faust*, and *Faust* took him a lifetime to write—nay, it was not finished when he died, for he corrected it every year. If, then, such a genius as Goethe could only produce one idea in a lifetime, it may be safely taken for granted that the common run of compilers cannot put more than one in each of their works. What an enormous amount of verbiage, then, must there be in a book of a thousand pages! Say that it took one hundred pages to give a fair description of the one original thought which prompted the author to commence, then there remain nine hundred pages, of thirty lines a page, and seven words a line, giving a total of one hundred and eighty-nine thousand waste words. *Faust*, which took a great genius, is not a long book either. The typical writer of our time, Charles Dickens, is the very impersonation of this verbiage and flow of words. His books, of five hundred closely-printed pages, in small type and double columns, are standing marvels of word-accumulations. Setting aside the cleverness of the author, what is it but one ceaseless flow of sentences? It is the newspaper correspondent spun out, and bound in three volumes. The competition is to pile up the greatest heaps and pyramids of words. So it is with our leaders of politics: the post can only be held by men who can talk, talk—talk, in good old homely phrase, 'a horse's head off.' That is the qualification for a statesman: neither talents, nor genius, nor research, but 'jaw.'

Louis got tired of his paper. Yet the *Pall Mall* is an honourable exception to the vast mass of verbiage poured out daily, almost hourly, by the metropolitan press. Here, at least, they condense the news, however dull and uninteresting it may be. But even here they are obliged, by custom, by the monstrous appetite for words, to print columns upon columns utterly idea-less, to coin a phrase. As for the leading daily paper, its contents every morning are equal in extent to a three-volume novel.

Louis yawned, and, leaning back against the side of the box, languidly fixed his eyes upon the profile of Heloise. The man could not make her out, nor himself out either. He was puzzled. He could not understand himself, and it made him irritable. He was irritable enough by nature, without this additional impetus. She worried him. He wished her out of sight every hour, and yet he was always studying her. They had been married about six weeks.

If he had been left to himself, he would have been on the Continent at that moment —it was just his favourite time. Not that he would have been anywhere in the usual and well-beaten track. It would not have been the Spa, or the roulette-table, or any of the other excuses for the congregation of human beings, that would have attracted him. He would have been in Antwerp. Did you ever see the picture of the interior of Antwerp Cathedral painted by a certain famous artist,

and now in a certain well-known gallery not
far from Landseer's dirty lions?   This picture
is not much noticed; there is never any
crowd about it. Yet it has a beauty which
is peculiarly its own.   The æsthetic nature of
the artist, the intense sensual spirituality of
his soul, live in this work.   It is a contradic-
tion in terms; but it is a fact that there is
such a thing as sensual spirituality. Here
you may see it.   The long dim arches of the
cathedral, solemn and still, are filled with an
undefined blue mist.   You cannot see this
blue mist if you look straight at it, or even
if you think of it, or search for it.   But it
grows out of the canvas as the gaze rests
upon it; it steals out from the dark places,
and clouds the outlines of the pillars till the
roof of the building floats upon azure colour.
The curve of the arch, the regularity of the
pillars, the beauty of the architecture, are
spiritual. This colour is sensual. The two
together form what can only be called a
sensual spiritualism; which is a union of the
beauty perceived by the chaste and some-

what sad mind and of the beauty which fascinates the eye. What a city must Antwerp be when the blue of heaven thus comes down and dwells in the holy places, as the Shechinah, the 'cloud,' rested upon the ark behind the curtains of the Tabernacle! A city pure and morally lovely thus to be honoured by the celestial ether!

Louis would laugh his horrid grating laugh, if he could read this. He had other ideas of Antwerp. He was aware of a certain street of palaces and temples, yea, verily, temples, devoted to the worship of a goddess, nameless now, but highly spoken of by those of olden time. An infamous place—infamous far and near—this street. Do not misjudge Louis so far as to think that he debased himself personally. But it was a congenial atmosphere. Men were to be met there who could not be seen elsewhere; and these men were—what? They deserve a chapter to themselves. If time allows, they shall have it. They are foremost in the van of progress without faith—progress without moral principle. Alison, the voluminous (I was about to say the *great*) historian, describes Napoleon I. as answering to the Christian's idea of the devil, *i.e.* supreme intellect without moral principle. These men are not Napoleons, but they influence the world collectively, and almost as much as he did. Yet they have no names, no cohesion—they are wandering individuals.

It was these men whose society Louis had loved. He was not quite certain whether he loved it still or not. But he called to mind the fact, that had it not been for Heloise he would have been among them at that hour. It was his time: when the nuts began to harden he took his way thither. He dwelt in memory upon the scenes he had witnessed, the *splendid* talk he had heard there; the splendid enchanting talk—so grand, so ignoble, so aspiring, yet so base and mean, but in all things novel, new, exciting! It was a San Francisco saloon minus the inevitable revolver. Louis was a coward; all advanced men are—that is, advanced men of *his* order. There are reasons for that, too. He dwelt still upon those scenes; they passed before his mind's eye. This was an evil thing for Heloise.

She did not disturb his billiards, or his club-dinner, or his card-party, or his wine, because he had no habits of that kind. She simply upset him from beginning to end. There was no personal inconvenience, no crossing of his purpose—for he had no purpose, no wilful interference with his pet pursuits, no demands upon his time. He recognised it at last. He discovered what it was. It was simply her presence that ruffled him. He could not sleep in self-contemplation while she was near; he could not close his eyes surrounded with troops of old and familiar ideas; her presence jarred, some how, upon him. The delicate sensitiveness of his inner being was continually irritated; like the gold leaf of an electronometer, his repose was perpetually disturbed by the influence that irradiated from her. He had an ever-increasing desire to be alone, and yet he could not leave her side. He groaned under the infliction of having to wait upon her, and yet he watched her slightest wish, and hastened to forestall it. He chafed, and yet he tried to persuade himself that he was calm—so calm, that he had settled down to a rationally happy existence.

He had not been to these theatres for ten years. The whole thing was familiar, and yet strange. Everything seemed the same; but he had changed. The glitter was gone; the charm had fled; the velvet had faded; the gilding was tarnished; the flaring gas was dim. It was equally faded and tarnished and dim ten years ago; but his mind was fresh then, his eye uncritical, his senses joying in light and colour and brilliance. The brightness and beauty of the thing was in his own soul, and he poured it out upon the theatre, and lit it up with the light of his own abundant spirit. But now the stage was wood, and the drama itself mere words without meaning—hollow sounds only; his own heart, in fact, was hollow and empty. He did not reason all this out, but the sense and feeling of it made him irritable. Heloise had brought him back into desert places; places he had reaped and garnered beforehand, and now they were barren and desolate. He had no complaint to make, and yet he was dissatisfied.

CHAPTER II.

It was only a little way out of the dusty highway, and yet it was a lovely spot. The road there was flat, and the scene tame and dull. There was an odour of stale beer and coarse tobacco, a stable-like smell, at the entrance to the village, which came from a low whitewashed public-house, where the teams stopped for refreshment. The carters drank from a great quart cup, and the horses drank a green unwholesome-looking liquor stagnating in a trough, and called by courtesy water, as the viler beverage was called beer, and each was about as muddy and thick as the other. Near the horse-trough, on one side, was a heap of manure, strewn with egg-shells and stumps of decaying cabbages and pea-pods, tainting the air still further; and on the other, a rude bench—a plank unplaned,

rough from the saw, supported on two unhewn logs. The end of the house faced the
road, and the thatch could be easily touched
by a man on horseback. There was one
small lattice-window, with three broken panes
at this end, close under the roof, and in this
window was a card with the inscription, 'Good
Ginger-beer sold here,' with a couple of black-
ing-bottles by way of illustration; for the
spruce glass bottles of 'aerated-waters' manu-
facturers had not penetrated so far as this
yet. This end of the house had a yellowish
unhealthy look; the whitewash was discoloured
with age and the weather. The place was
overshadowed with a great horse-chestnut-
tree, whose brown-and-yellow leaves and the
prickly cases of its fruit strewed the ground.
It was a noble tree, utterly inappropriate to
such a place; the very contrast, in its glorious
growth and beautiful proportions, to the coarse
rudeness of the house, and the people who
stayed there beneath its shade. In the spring,
when the clusters of blossom hung upon each
bough till the whole tree looked like a splendid

candelabra—each blossom a lamp—the contrast was almost painful. It seemed as if the jests and the oaths, and the rank smell of beer and horses, must pollute it; but, utterly unconscious of the foulness surrounding it, the tree grew and flourished in calm splendour, in conscious superiority, unmoved. 'I am not of thine order. I do not sneer at or condemn thee and such as thee, thou rude and coarse boor at my foot; but I soar upwards, and I put forth things of beauty, and I rejoice in the sun and the wind and the rain, and the sight of the sky above me, and of the stars by night. Thus absorbed I neither see, nor hear, nor am conscious of the human miasma beneath me. A time shall come— only once perhaps in my whole lifetime—when a traveller, journeying hither, and sore bruised in spirit, but noble at heart, shall gaze upon me and my flower-lamps, and, strengthened thereby, yield no more to the depressing influence of the dusty ways of life, but hold on his road with quickened step, seeking the true and the beautiful.'

The muddy beer dulled their hearing, and they never guessed that the tree was thus speaking. This was the Sun Inn, at Avonbourne. On the blue ground of the sign there was painted a round human face, with goggling eyes and open mouth, and surrounded with sharp rays all in brightest yellow. This represented the sun—the wondrous orb of day, theme of the poets, supporter of life, the god Ra of the Egyptians, thus insulted and brought down to the level of the minds of the carters and ploughmen, who hailed it as the assurance of beer. They have taught us from our youth up to despise the idolaters of the bygone ages. We spit upon them, and cry, 'Poor wretches, miserable creatures!' But see here. Reflect upon the grandeur and majesty of the sun, the king of heaven, the centre upon which all earthly life depends, the giver of heat and light—light, the noblest of all material things; is not the sun the very highest triumph of the Creator's art— the *chef-d'œuvre* of Heaven? Is it not an ever-present witness to the inscrutable God? And degraded to an alehouse sign, represented in such rude conventional style as the very aborigines of America, the most uncultivated savages, could easily surpass! The carters and the ploughmen fling stones at it, and guffaw as a flint strikes the flat nose, or open mouth, or glaring insane eyes. Consider: are they not more ignorant than the idolaters who knelt to the sun as the visible sign of God in the ages long ago? Have they a right to cast a sneer upon the Magi—a right to repeat Sunday anathemas upon the idolaters?

There were a few houses right and left of this inn. They do not concern us. But there was a lane in front of the Sun, and this lane led to the beautiful and lovely spot where Heloise was born. Who, sojourning an hour at that inn, under the shade of the chestnut-tree, would have suspected it?—for though the downs were near they appeared brown and parched, nothing lovely.

Winding and turning, the lane came down to the bourne. The swallows ga-

thered thickly in the osier beds at this time.
The tall yellow rods of willow were black
with the folded wings of the birds of summer,
as they lit down upon them in countless
crowds, and, pruning their feathers, chattered
incessantly of the voyage they soon must
take. How busy those little brains must be!
how those little minds must work, and try
to think of this and that! how the tiny bills
open and shut perpetually as they pour their
ideas out in a ceaseless stream of eloquence!
O, for a shorthand reporter who understood
the language of birds! what a newspaper that
would be which he could write! Wherever
the beggars find an open door and generous
hearts ready to give, there they set up a mark
upon the wall that the next passer-by may
know he is sure of his reception. The fowls
of the air do likewise; only we cannot see
their marks. They gather where the human
inhabitants are kindly-hearted. Those who
live in the country know that there are wide
tracts where birds are rarely seen, even
woods unpeopled with songsters; and there

are spots where they crowd together, and in one single orchard specimens of almost the whole tribe can be found. Why is this? There is some secret invisible chord of sympathy. Pierce Lestrange said the birds came about his home because he never offended the fairies. This was Heloise's father. It was his poetical way of expressing the fact that he lived in accord with nature. Wherever men swear and fight, wherever houses are unnaturally crowded together, and an unnatural course of living is followed, almost everywhere where brick and mortar come, from thence the fairies fly away never to return. But Pierce would have no lonely dell or woody nook of his land defiled that he might make 'filthy lucre.' Therefore the birds gathered about that place. He would not have the swallows' nests disturbed under his eaves; no nest was ever taken in his precincts. The great thrush—the missel-thrush—wildest and fiercest of all its class, untamable, unsociable, had built for twenty years every spring in the yew-tree just in

front of the breakfast-parlour window. That
tree was his inheritance. The thrush of that
day had inherited it from his father, and he
again from his grandfather—three genera-
tions. Very jealous the thrush was, too, of his
domain; no other bird dared build in that tree,
no other dared even perch upon the branches,
if he, the lord and master, was there. The
cooing of the wild doves was heard the whole
day long in the great chestnut-trees at the
lower end of the garden. The starlings
marched to and fro upon the lawn; the
blackbird washed himself in the fountain before the door, fearless, unhesitatingly. On
the wall of the garden the peacock, slowly
and stately, stepped up and down, spreading
abroad his wealth of colour. The rabbits
had ventured in and burrowed under the
rhododendrons ; they peeped forth in the
evening, in the dusk, frisking their white tails
in joy of life. The goldfinches sang in the
morning on the apple-trees—trees which grew
almost under Pierce's window. 'I could not
be happy,' he said, 'unless I heard the finches

sing when I wake.' He was an old man, too, of seventy, and very gray; yet such was his pleasure in living creatures. The butterflies were always in that garden; the humming-bird moths came to the geraniums; the hum of the bees rose and fell perpetually as the tiny insects flew hurriedly by ; the restless wasps were hard at work on the plums now —for Pierce had fruit-trees all round the walls of his garden, in the centre of which was a wide lawn, and in the centre of that a vast thicket of rhododendrons and laurel, where the rabbits hid themselves. The orchard branched out at one side, and at the very end of the lawn the bourne, the stream flowing towards the Avon, wound along. A treacherous bank it was, for the water-rats, undisturbed, had bored it with innumerable tunnels—utterly undisturbed, let alone to do as they pleased. Bold and timid too they were. A movement, a wave of the hand, the slightest sound, and splash they had dived out of sight. But remain still and silent, and in a moment or two a brown head peeped out, a black eye twinkled; out came the miniature beaver, and, seating himself upon his hinder part, washed his face with his tiny paws. The stream ran deep and strong here, under this bank towards the lawn, so deep that the eye could not penetrate its depth; but out yonder, half-way across to the other side, one could see the waving weeds, slowly vibrating along their length to the motion of the water. Here the still patient pike lay motionless for hours, awaiting his prey—the roach, who restlessly swam to and fro in the black pool under the lawn bank, seen occasionally as they turned sideways and showed their white glancing under part. Thence it shallowed till the mud appeared, where the marks of the moor-hen's foot could be traced, and the flags grew green in the spring with yellow flowers; the iris, now brown and withered, rustling in the breeze. There, too, grew the tall reeds, with their graceful flower-bunches; and beyond these the bank rose high, and over it was a belt of impervious fir-trees and pines, scenting the air with their exuding gum, and bearing cones high up towards the topmost branches.

This was Pierce's garden—or rather this is a dim outline of it; for it contained inexhaustible riches of this kind. The downs rose up a short distance beyond the bourne—downs upon whose slopes you might lie, and listen to the whistling of the breezes through the bennets, till all thought of the world and its contentions passed out of the mind. The old house rambled about, like Pierce's mind, and yet was substantial and large, and even stately after its way. These had been abbey lands, and one small portion of the abbey itself remained, and was built upon and all round by those who erected the mansion. This was the breakfast-parlour, Pierce's favourite room, with the great yew-tree shadowing its mullioned window, and the walls wainscoted, and the furniture of oak, fantastically carved, as no man carves in this our day: at once grim, grotesque, and artistic, there are none who can grave in such guise now. Somewhat sombre was this room; there was an air of slumberous age about it. Here he had brought some of the treasures from the old abbey library. There was the ponderous chartulary, yellow with age, lying, of all places, upon the sideboard; and close by it curious folios upon astrology, and the rare and precious early tomes of Shakespeare; these all scattered about, as novels and such works are in ordinary rooms. He said that he liked this free confusion better than the formal stateliness of a library. His guests were free to open and to read a few lines just as they pleased, or to entirely pass the treasures by; there was no ceremonious unlocking of cases, no careful handling, no show. The other window of the room, which looked out upon the orchard, and by which there ran a path, he had filled with ancient glass, taken from a chapel in the old abbey. The central figure of the window, in bright and yet mellow colour, was a cardinal blessing with the two uplifted fingers and the extended thumb of the Roman Church. Near by were saints and angels, with faces familiar as those of the carters and ploughboys—

homely and yet lifelike; portraits of men
whom the ancient artist had known, and whom
he had crowned in the Heaven of his fancy.
This was not one design; it was composed of
pieces from several windows—all that had
been preserved—arranged with no view except to have the most brilliant colours, such
as the cardinal's hat, in the centre. The lands
were purchased in Queen Elizabeth's time
from one of King Henry VIII.'s favourites,
who had had them almost a free gift when that
monarch dissolved the monasteries. Pierce's
ancestor of that day had been a judge, and he
was the grandest of the family; there had
been none with any worldly ambition since.
They had one and all refused to be made more
than magistrates; one and all they had kept
out of politics; one and all they had farmed
a good share of the estates themselves. These
were not large, but large enough to place
them in the position of country gentlemen.
Pierce more than all the rest lived in seclusion, yet spent the whole of his income. True,
that income was hardly more than half what

he could rightfully have claimed. He had surrendered the other portion to his younger brother, in order that he might remain near him. Philip lived barely a bowshot distant, in a house known as the Vicarage; for Pierce was the lay impropriator, and took the great tithes. This was a more modern mansion, square and compact. A broad paved footpath ran straight from one house to the other; half-way it was parted with a door arched in the wall; beyond this was another paved footpath, running at right angles, and then a second door opening into Philip's garden. These doors were never locked, but they were there. The paved footpath running at right angles went down the hill somewhat to the church where Philip officiated, whose low tower was hidden by the chestnut-trees.

Why was it that the barns of the place were always full? Why was it that the sun seemed ever to shine here, and even the storm, when it came, was altogether lovely? For the coloured bow gleamed out from the

angry cloud, and rested its ethereal arch—
the portal of heaven—upon the everlasting
hills, and smiling peace was there again.
Nature dealt lovingly with the old man
Pierce—most lovingly of all in giving him
Heloise.

He had married in his youth; what
came of that does not matter in this place.
He had married again in his middle age
— married a French lady too, above all
things, as the neighbours sneered; and what
came of that was Heloise. The mother was
long dead. It had been left to Pierce to
watch the peach ripen, to see the bloom
gather upon the rind, and the delicate tints
and velvety softness grow to surpassing
beauty.

She was hardly strong enough even now
to carry him the abbey chartulary from the
shelf to his chair: a delicate slight girl, not
tall, and yet not short; delicate as the richest
exotic, and yet all impulse, all nervous excitement. Perfectly healthy, the doctor said
—perfectly healthy; but beware how she was

shocked. As long as she was happy she would flourish; but the winter of sorrow, if such should come, would most assuredly kill her. He had kept that winter away as yet. Her bird-like movements had never been fettered with the dull clog of misery. She danced about the house from morning till night; she rode, she sang, she played, happy as the day was long. The long curling black hair was rarely confined with band or ribbon; it flowed freely upon her shoulders in luxuriant wilfulness, and clung around her neck in ringlets. The long, long eyelashes drooped upon her cheek, half-hiding the eye, even when wide open. They were large eyes—large and liquid—of the deepest azure blue. The eyebrows were narrow, black, and well marked, not too arched; the complexion dazzlingly white— white as the driven snow—with the faintest flush of colour, like a blush rose, in the cheek. But the mouth — who shall describe the mouth? Mobile and ever-changing, its expression never fixed, what artist could ever hope to transfer those lips to the canvas? It pouted, and it looked lovely; it smiled, and enchanted; there was a flash of momentary anger, and it bewitched you. Her soul ever hovered near her lips.

‘ Sweet Helen makes me immortal with a kiss ;
Her lips draw forth my soul : see where it flies.’

Pierce in his inmost communings ever thought of her as Psyche; but she was too lively for the conventional conception of Psyche—never still; ever in motion; always eager for change and excitement. Other people remarked this, and said slightingly that it was a sign of her French extraction. One thing only ever kept her still—one thought only ever made her silent and reflective; it was religion. She could not have told you why, but the feeling of religion was ingrained in her very inmost being. It was a peculiar religion, it is true; an æsthetic longing rather than a tangible realisation. It had no existence apart from colour and light and joy. So she was rarely seen at church; it was too cold and damp and dim and dull there. It was all stone—dead.

Other people said this, too, was the result of
her French extraction. As the tree, so the
fruit; as the mother was Roman Catholic, the
child would not go to a Protestant church.
This was harsh and untrue; she had been
carefully bred up in the Protestant faith. It
was not that; it was the lack of life at the
church. There was no sunshine in it, no
colour, no light. Heloise's heart was full of
aspirings—after she knew not what, but which
she deemed were sacred hopes. She sat under
the old chestnut-trees, watching the shadows
dancing, and let these feelings have their
way. She climbed up the steep-sided downs,
and, choosing a hollow sheltered from the
wind, lay down upon the soft thymy turf,
while the bees flew overhead and the lark
sang high above her, and dreamt day-dreams,
not of heaven, but of something—she knew
not what; of a state of existence all and every
hour of which should be light and joy and
life. It was one of her fancies, this lying on
the broad earth, with her ear close to the
ground, that she could feel the heart of the

world throb slowly far underneath. Pierce,
living himself among the classics, desired that
she should share his pleasures, and had put
English translations of them into her hands;
and it was perhaps from these, from old Dioge-
nes Laertius or Plato, that these fancies had
their birth; for some of these old philosophers
taught that the world collectively was in itself
a vast animal or creature, with heart and pulse
and soul. In the silence of the hills she could
hear this great heart throb. She was on these
hills often in the very early morning, riding
her pony, and watching the light and shadow
as the sun rose over the clouds of mist.
Pierce encouraged her in this; the air did her
good. It was the air, the physicians said, which
made her, though so delicate, yet so healthy,
so to say, so full of life. But the evening was
her favourite time, when the sunset flamed in
the west, one gorgeous mass of gold and crimson and brilliant hues. She would slowly
ride about till the first planet shone forth,
and then homeward with a gentle and chas-
tened feeling, sending up, it might be, from her

heart a prayer to the Heaven she had been taught to believe in.

Looking at her from our distance, calmly and critically, the question arises, Was she or was she not a pagan?

It was a religion that mingled with every hour of her daily life—no matter of one hour every week, but an ever-present reality. Once more, this was Heloise's home, these were the influences under which she grew up. She had seen nothing of life, nothing of society. Her time had been passed in this 'dull country house.' What wonder that she entered so eagerly into the excitement of the theatre? She was so absorbed with the rapid changes of the six weeks they had been married, she never even suspected Louis of sneering. She did not detect the faint inflection of his tone of voice; she was unconscious of his mockery. Louis, remember, was outwardly attentive and considerate to a fault. She was too excited for even her sensitive nature to as yet feel the jar —to recognise the barely-perceptible shadow which had already fallen across her path.

Sweet Heloise—married but six weeks—even her best and sweetest temper was of no avail. Unseen, the gold of the wedding-ring was tarnishing already.

CHAPTER III.

A FATALIST, as all close observers of Nature and all *intense* minds are, Pierce traced the loss of Heloise to that first unfortunate marriage of his. This was why he had kept her in such strict seclusion. He argued with himself—told himself that it was for her health; it was better that she should not be excited; in his heart of hearts he well knew that he dreaded her entrance into society, lest she should marry, and leave him. He could not contemplate the possibility of so lovely a creature passing unnoticed amidst the crowd; she would be sure to be snatched away from him, and he should be left alone. Therefore he had kept her in the country, tortured at times with the fear lest he was doing her an injustice, doubting whether, in his selfishness, he was not injuring her, whom he loved above all. But he could not bring himself to part with her, not even for three months. It would have been different, he said, if she had pined for change, if she had panted for the legitimate pleasures and amusements of youth. But Heloise, so impetuous and so fond of motion, never showed the least inclination to leave him, never asked to go out into the world. She was contented, happy ; and he was only too glad that she should be so. Now he traced events back to their beginning, and saw, or thought he saw, that the very precautions he had taken to secure her to himself had resulted in precisely the opposite manner to what he had hoped and intended. It was fate.

Not the Fate conceived of by the ancients —the overwhelming Necessity, which could not be withstood, even by the gods; but to which they, too, must succumb. Even in our modern Christian and civilised, let us add sceptical, time, such a Necessity is partly acknowledged. For the great Founder of the Christian religion, in the agony of the moment, cried out that if possible the supreme hour of torture might be averted. But no; not even for Him could the irresistible march of events be stayed! It was not the Fate that drove the hero of Sophocles' saddest drama to kill his father, and wed his mother in mental blindness. Nor did Pierce recognise the so-called 'Providence' which in our modern tongue is the synonym of the 'destiny' and the 'fate' of the olden times. What he meant by fate was the singular and unexpected con-catenation of circumstances which human in-genuity could not foresee. Cæsar Borgia said that he had foreseen the death of his father, he had calculated on that; he had foreseen the animosity of the cardinals, and had cal-culated the required amount of counter-action; he had foreseen that the troops would desert him. He had taken measures to overcome all these difficulties. But he had *not* foreseen that he should be ill himself, and incapable of action. That ruined him. They show a tower in a city of the west of England, and they call it a 'Folly,' because it was built by a man to shield his only son and heir from the death, by bite of an adder, which was foretold by the astrologers. The boy was kept in the tower night and day, and the father rejoiced, and cried, 'He is safe.' But in the course of time the servants took in some fagots of wood for fuel, and in those fagots was an adder, which crept out and stung the lad. Therefore they call it a 'Folly,' as showing that human wisdom is weak and powerless to control the great Unknown.

Pierce had taught Heloise to find pleasures and joys where girls of her age would usually see nothing but dulness and inanity. He had shown her heart-stirring things in the woods, the downs, the sky, and in the very grass under her feet. For he said, 'If she joys in these, she will never leave me; she will never hanker after the artificial.' He had built up a tower around her to bind her in and secure her, and now he found it a 'folly.'

It was his first marriage. It came up even at this distance of time, and flung itself in his teeth. Yet there was nothing criminal in it either; nothing even inappropriate, as far as man could see; they were fairly matched, to all appearance: but it was a mistake. In the sight of the irresistible laws which govern the universe, a mistake is as fruitful of evil effects as the greatest of all crimes. Out of that marriage Louis came to Avonbourne. Yet how he came seemed wrapped in a dense mist of obscurity. Pierce never could see the reason as to why and wherefore. He came out of a cloud. Nothing very obscure either, looking at it in a commonplace way. Carlotta came, and with her her husband and Louis.

Carlotta, Pierce's eldest daughter, by his first wife. But why should she come that spring to visit her old home? The answer is simple enough. It may sound strange, but this man, her father, only knew her features from a miniature painted ten years ago. He had not seen her since her childhood. She had passed from his sphere as a girl—a wilful, pettish, ambitious, artificial creature. Pierce's garden was not for her. She found friends easily with her relations; they brought her up. And this was how it was. She never came back—not once in full five-and-twenty years. For a whole quarter of a century he never saw her face. She left him at fifteen, she came back at forty—came back, unexpected, unannounced, one lovely evening in spring. With her Louis *and* her husband, or her husband *and* Louis—which you please. She had married early, and wondrously well, as every one said she would. At twenty she went to the altar with one whom Mammon favoured as a man 'after his own heart.' A bullionist, a discounter of bills, in Lombard-street; on the Continent, a raiser of loans for tottering governments, a master in their secret councils. Personally a man of polished steel. Not brazen, or loud, or oily, or canting, nor 'gentlemanly' only; but of polished steel. A light spare form, well proportioned; a handsome face, only expressionless; a low voice, but a voice which you could hear at double the distance of the hissing thick sounds which issue from the great majority of throats; polished and hard — such was

Horton Knoyle of Knoyle. He was no vulgar speculator on the Exchange, no fortune-hunter, but a prince—a prince by reason of his power, a prince by reason of his aristocratic position. Carlotta, in a single step, rose to a sphere where she could not see Pierce. He passed away entirely. Ambassadors, dukes, princes of the blood, sovereigns —these were her guests, these her hosts, now. The garden at Avonbourne sank into the ground and was hidden. After her marriage her portrait was painted in oil by a famous artist; from this a miniature was taken, and sent to Pierce by the aunt who had brought her up, who had launched her into 'society,' as a sort of triumph. It represented Carlotta in full dress, wearing her diamonds—the Knoyle diamonds. Pierce was not asked to the wedding. The country gentry poured in to congratulate him; he received them with exquisite politeness, but he was silent. They saw they should get no *entrée* into a higher class through him, and the subject dropped. Carlotta passed out of sight. Now and then

they saw in the papers that such and such
a grand reception had been held by Lady
Knoyle; for she was a peeress in her own right
now. Horton refused the minister's offer
for himself, but, as the papers said, gracefully
placed the coronet upon his consort's head.
If any man could have seen into his heart
as he did so! Excepting these notices there
was an utter blank between the parent and the
daughter.

Till all at once she and Knoyle and Louis
came to Avonbourne in the still May eve—
in early May, before the June roses had
shown their opening buds. Without a note
of warning, without a letter giving notice of
their approach—as if Bourne Manor was an
hotel—superciliously they came. Till the
carriage stopped at the hall-door no one knew
of their coming. Pierce and Heloise were
out riding at the hour. They entered; Carlotta took her old rooms; they unpacked their
luggage, sent the horses to the stable, ordered
refreshment, and calmly awaited the return
of their host. Pierce had often pictured to

himself a meeting with his long-lost daughter;
he felt that his limbs would tremble when he
did see her at last. Now she had come, he
met her, kissed her, talked to her as if she
had been the most ordinary visitor. He expressed no surprise at their coming—he made
them welcome. He was far too highly-bred
to show the least resentment at the cool
supercilious manner in which he had been
treated. He accompanied Horton that very
evening to the famous trout-preserve on the
estate, producing the fishing-tackle as if he
had been his son-in-law's gamekeeper. He
showed Horton how to fish. This man of
steel had been advised to try trout-fishing as
a relief to the mind! It was the first time he
had ever held a rod. This was ostensibly the
reason of their arrival: Horton was over-
worked — wanted rest, the physicians said,
and prescribed him country air and fishing.
Horton smiled, and did as they bid. But
there was fishing enough elsewhere — why
Avonbourne was chosen was Carlotta's affair.
Also trout-fishing was not the cause of Louis

accompanying them. And Heloise all this time? Heloise was never tired of watching her half-sister. She would gaze at her almost for hours at a time. She could not understand her; she was a creature so totally distinct from aught she had ever imagined or seen. Carlotta was an enigma to her.

Oddly enough, Pierce and Louis became great friends—rather let us say great talkers together. Perhaps it was the extreme contrast between their habits of thought. In their mode of life they had been the antipodes of each other. Each in his peculiar way and in his own particular walk had been a great observer. Only Pierce observed the workings of the laws of God with a reverential feeling; Louis had watched the ways of men with ever-increasing scepticism. Pierce knew Nature; Louis knew man. There was much that was utterly repulsive to Pierce in Louis' expressions, in his tone, his whole style of life. But the old man made allowances for the different calibre of his guest. He tried to imagine himself in the other's place, with completely opposite tastes, inclinations; under a widely-varying chain of circumstances; exposed to influences which he had never felt the power of. He subtracted all the dross, and threw it on one side, and believed that there still remained no little ore at the bottom. It was Pierce's own generous and noble way of estimating men.

There was something singularly interesting in Louis' conversation; not the talk of the drawing-room, but his talk when he was alone with men. He had seen so much of human nature under such exceptional conditions, he had a caustic epigrammatic method of condensing his bitter truths into sharp arrowy sentences, that left a sting, as it were, behind. He had travelled widely, and travelled in out-of-the-way and unvisited places. But it was never among the woods and forests and seas. He had never penetrated the primeval forest; never sailed on the unknown seas, or felt the simoom in the midst of the desert. These were not what he had sought. It was always cities, never

Nature, that he had visited, and sojourned within. And such places within those cities as the world never dreamed existed upon the earth: the lowest beerhouse, the most miserable estaminet, the worst, the dirtiest, the most criminal and abandoned districts. Not that he lowered himself to intoxication, or to still worse pleasures in those sties of iniquity. He did not go there for what others went; he visited them to watch, and study the habits and thoughts of those who frequented the place for the gratification of their desires. As the student of medicine and surgery is made acquainted with the filthiest and most repulsive phases of disease, so Louis studied the most loathsome and coarsely *outré* states of life, not that he might gain an insight, or learn a lesson from which to teach or better mankind, but simply and solely from a desire—a craving unnatural desire—to see man in his 'nakedness.' Not the nakedness of the body, but the exposure of the animal instincts, the hate, the cruelty, the avarice, and the lust. He would stand for hours by the bar of the lowest public-house, sipping a single glass of weak brandy-and-water, lazily watching out of his half-closed eyes the motions, or listening to the talk, of the brutes in human form who made that house their chief resort. With the microscope of his mind he dissected the characters of these creatures—they cannot be called men.

This was a strange occupation for a peer of England; for Louis was a peer, though he rarely used the title.

What reason was there for this morbid frame of mind? Was it that he was dimly conscious of his own unutterable baseness, of the total lack of moral consciousness within him, that led him to take a miserable pleasure in thus proving to his own satisfaction that such was the normal condition of mankind? But this was not all that he had seen. By the aid of the acquaintances picked up in these dens of infamy, he had penetrated into fraternities whose very existence was utterly unsuspected; even into that most secret and nameless band some of whose members could be found at

Antwerp in the autumn of the year. Here
he had learnt strange and startling novelties
of thought; here he had seen and studied
men whose minds and lives marked them out
as distinctly as if they had been inhabitants
of another world. He knew curious secrets
of the Commune, of the societies that still
pester the peace of the Continent. In one
word, he knew as no other man did the
weird, the bizarre, and the devilish in human
life.

This man became Pierce's constant companion—Pierce the mild, the gentle, and the
blameless. It was the fascination of his talk
which threw a light over him. It was the
novelty, the utter antithesis. It was the
opportunity for a study which had never
occurred to Pierce, the great student, before.
It was reading the 'world' as in a book.
Through it all Louis made him and others
feel that whatever he had seen, whatever he
had heard, he, Louis, remained undefiled, an
English gentleman still. That this was the
case his manner was strong testimony—ele-

gant, and gentlemanly polite, pleasant; ever ready to forward the amusement of others.

This man, of all others, married Heloise. Looking back afterwards Pierce said it was occasioned by his 'folly'—his endeavour to keep her to himself by secluding her. She had seen so little of the world, she had had no variety to choose from. Carlotta encouraged the match. Horton left them long before anything of this was talked of—went back to his bullion, his bills, his loans; silent as to where his care laid—here or there. Carlotta remained. She and Louis and Heloise went about together as brother and sisters. They rode together; they rambled upon the hills; always these three—never Louis and Carlotta alone, never Heloise and Louis alone. There was nothing in this that any one could disapprove of. But yet at times Pierce felt that there was a chord of sympathy —a faint invisible connection—between Carlotta and Louis which he could not understand. Their bearing towards each other was haughty and distant; yet they were, it seemed, ever animated by the same impulses. It only occurred to him at times; it was a passing impression — a dream that came and went, and left no tangible mark behind. He was glad, or professed to be glad—tried to argue himself into being glad—that Carlotta and Heloise were so friendly. It was a reunion after so many years. It was as it ought to be.

Carlotta was very generous over the marriage. She presented Heloise with a magnificent set of diamonds; she showered presents upon her; she clothed her in garments of priceless value, till Heloise cried out shrinkingly that these things were not meet for her. Her innate modesty arose, and for the time overcame the natural vanity of a mere child; for she was but nineteen. But Carlotta, the subtle, over-persuaded her, and she accepted them, as she had accepted Louis—partly, at least—at Carlotta's hands.

After the wedding the bride and bridegroom went to the Lakes; after that to London, at Heloise's own special desire.

CHAPTER IV.

AT least Louis believed he loved her. It was the fact, at any rate, that he had felt towards her as he had felt towards no other human being before. No other emotion had ever occurred to him that he could not analyse, that he could not destroy with merciless criticism — not sparing himself. But Heloise exercised an influence over him which he could not analyse. It hurried him on too rapidly. She was the last that, in his calmer moments, he would have chosen—the last that he had ever pictured to himself as occupying the position of his wife. Like all other men who belong, in however distant a manner, to his class, Louis avoided the idea of a wife. It was synonymous, in his accepted creed, with innumerable vexations to which no reasonable man could submit. But she had swept away these thoughts—subverted the order of his mind. The idea of vexation, of annoyance, never entered his mind as possible in connection with her during that brief period of wild dreaming at Avonbourne— wild, inasmuch as it carried away the reflective portion of the man. It was the highest elevation that Louis ever reached in his whole moral existence. The dormant soul, latent even in the sceptical, reasoning, questioning, ever-doubting Pyrrhonist, rose to the surface—struggled itself out, attracted by the magnetism of Heloise's wondrous beauty and purity. For a brief period it raised itself in conquest over the mind and the brain, over the accumulated doubt of years. The soul stood confessed in the man who disbelieved in its existence. Louis' whole being was wrapped up in her for those three or four months in the natural life at Avonbourne. He believed he loved her. Those who knew his previous course would have pronounced love impossible to him. To us, however, judging him impartially, it is clear that for

the hour and the day Louis did love Heloise
with the whole force of the divine passion.
Her single face, her single person, was power-
ful enough to overcome the influences which
had been growing up around him for years.
Her voice overcame the sophistries of the hundreds with whom he had conversed; it penetrated to his very heart.

And Heloise? She knew nothing of love,
so to say. She had had no experience in
these things. An innocent girl, hardly out
of her childhood, pure of heart and mind, secluded from all society, how should she learn
to analyse her feelings, and to distinguish between the real emotion and the transient
excitement? One thing she, in all her innocence, could not help seeing—Louis' wildest,
blindest admiration of her. Inexperienced,
and uneducated in the science of the heart,
those symptoms thrilled a chord that existed
somewhere in her own bosom. The necessity
to love and to be loved existed in her heart;
he caused that string to vibrate, and how was
she to distinguish whether or no his was the

master-hand, if he only could play it aright?
Shall we confess that Heloise, in her girlish
way, felt a little proud of her lover? Will that
lower her in one's estimation? It was so natural in a girl so much secluded, so purely
unartificial. She could not help a little, just
a little, warmth of pleasure in the thought
that this man of the world should see anything to admire in *her*. This very pride in
his admiration arose out of the low value she
put upon herself. A man of the world—there
was no little charm in that. So deep, so profound and original a thinker as he seemed to
be to her—such an apostle, as it were, of a
state of things and a mode of thought of
which previously she had had no conception
—he dazzled her.

So, too, he dazzled Pierce. Yet Pierce
had twinges of misgiving. But Carlotta
wound him about with her logic of society.
This man was a great match. He was rich,
he was titled, he had high connections. Such
an opportunity would never again happen to
the humble dwellers in Bourne Manor. It

would be a lasting honour to the family. The man himself, too, had sown his wild oats. He was old enough to settle down into a good and affectionate husband. It was evident how deeply he loved her. Subtle Carlotta went one step farther. She just hinted something more—she did not say so plainly, but she suggested the idea to Pierce's mind that unless the offer was accepted Heloise would never have another chance of rising to her half-sister's elevated position. This decided Pierce. Heloise must be as high as Carlotta. His tender and affectionate mind felt a jealous ambition for her. Yes: the offer must be accepted.

Easy it is now to understand why Heloise was so happy at the Haymarket. It was fairyland to her. These things, these sights and scenes and amusements, long over-done and nauseous to a satiated appetite, were new and entrancing to her. How she entered into the excitement of the hour! her heart, glowing with delight, expressing unaffected admiration.

This gushing palled upon Louis. He

argued with himself that it was right and proper and best that it should be so. It was better that his wife should be pure, fresh, and innocent; he could trust her. As a refined student of human nature, he should, even in his most passionless moments, have chosen a new heart, so to say—one on which no self-imposed task of deceit had as yet stamped its mark. It was the greatest safeguard against those follies and those vexations which married life is certain to bring in its wake. He could mould her, too, as he pleased. Thus he tried to deceive himself—to argue his own mind into satisfaction. How many thousands of us are, at this moment, earnestly engaged in the same attempt! And as soon as we have partially succeeded, we shut our eyes and slumber, as if sleep could assure us protection from the rising storm— as if the lightning would pass us over. Sharp is the awakening from this somnolency.

This perpetual gushing he tried to call in his own mind the natural and healthy delight of a new heart. But the very term

'gushing' would recur to his mind. He
could not help but note it—it palled upon
him. Gradually and imperceptibly it engen-
dered a contemptuous feeling — a sense of
superiority. At Avonbourne she had appeared so superior to him. Now he slowly
grew conscious of a species of superiority
which he possessed over her. By degrees he
came to criticise and analyse her, to watch
her face, to study her mind and her ways.
The result was the production of a process of
drawing parallelisms between her ·and those
low and brutal characters which he had lived
amongst so long. Heloise compared to them
—Heloise the pure at heart, the unaffected,
the natural, the very type of the creature
that 'thinketh no evil'—compared with the
ruffians of the gambling saloons, and a paral-
lelism instituted between her and such as
they were! Louis argued in this way : she
has the same instincts as they have. How
greatly she enjoyed the fragrant bouquet of
the priceless wines he set before her, novel,
and unknown to her palate before—wines un-

heard of in the simple life at Avonbourne! It was true that she drank but the merest drop—the sipping of a bird was not more in *amount*, but the *pleasure* was there equally, and was perhaps more than if she had partaken largely. These shows and theatres—see how her eyes sparkled as they entered the glittering palaces of the drama and the song! Different in degree, it was the same in kind with the maddening enthusiasm of the wildest San Franciscan frequenter of the lowest theatrical saloon — subdued, toned down, it might be; but still she possessed the same animal instincts as the rest of common humanity. Had she been exposed to the vile influences that other unfortunate women had been, doubtless she would have succumbed as they had done, and become the most degraded of all spectacles. Mark this: Louis always assumed the possibility of the good deteriorating to the bad. He never gave a thought to the equal possibility that the wicked and the degraded would have been honest and true had they enjoyed the same favourable conditions. Thus in these speculations he carried out his old habit of studying the worst side of human nature. He reduced Heloise, in the abstract, to the level of the pariahs of society.

Contempt for her grew by degrees into contempt for himself. He looked back upon that dream at Avonbourne as a species of insanity. He sneered at the recollection of himself. All the old habits rose up strong and irresistible in his heart. He yearned to go back to himself again ; for she had partially, and for a time, drawn him out of himself, made him for a while, at least, recognise that another human being had feelings and hopes and joys. But he could not remain thus. All the old instincts, all the habits acquired in so many years of perfect freedom, pulled and dragged at him harder and fiercer every day. They would not be denied. He felt it to be a bondage to be always with her. Though he had nothing to do, even if he omitted all those tender cares and little kindly efforts for her pleasure—as he began to omit them now—still there remained her presence, in itself a weariness to the flesh. He grew to detest the sight and sound of her. He chose a solitary room, and restlessly fidgeted at the echo of her approaching footstep. He was always occupied when she came near to him. He did not wish to be disturbed. He, who had never done an hour's work in his life, began to be full of business—important business that could not be delayed, that must be attended to, that required absolute solitude and silence, that made him irritable when intruded on, even by her, his dear Heloise.

It was long before she noticed the change that had come over him. She accepted his explanation in all good faith—she attributed all his irritable ways and desire to be away from her to the cares of business. She had a dim kind of idea that every man had a business to attend to. She never thought of doubting him. But when this went on for weeks, when she found herself, night after night, alone in the box at the theatre, a sense of loneliness, almost a sense of a wrong done to her, stole over her mind. She made no complaint; she did not even hint at her disappointment; but she tried, with unwearied attention, to win him back to her side. It was her own fault, she said to herself; she had enjoyed the change and the excitement and the amusement too much; she had neglected him. She ceased to go to the theatres, and came and sat with Louis. This made it ten times worse. Secretly, as soon as her carriage had left, he had of late gone out into the town, always returning before the time when she would return. He wished to be free of her company. Now she came and forced herself upon him. For an evening or two he bore it, without outward show, beyond an ill-suppressed restlessness. Even at the last he could not boldly say out that he wished to be alone. There was something about this girl, in her purity and her innocence, which made it impossible to insult her, or even to openly wound her. The third evening he left the room for a moment, and never returned. She did not see him till breakfast; still in her own mind she did not accuse him. The scales were long in falling from her eyes—so implicitly had she believed every word that fell from him at Avonbourne, so carefully had she treasured up the memory of those impassioned tones. But this occurred again and again.

She was always alone now. She could not go out, and enjoy herself as before. A heavy dulness began to overshadow her. The presence of a trouble never left her. Her wild and impetuous spirits fell. At last she realised the fact that he avoided her, that he wished her at a distance. Then she had a hard and wretched task. It was to keep away from him, and yet not to seem to avoid him of her own accord; to watch his mood, to be ready at any moment to please him, and yet at the same time not to interfere with his habits.

Why did she not go to Carlotta—her elder sister, the woman of the world, skilled in men and their ways? Might she not have obtained assistance there?

Heloise could not tell why, but although this resource had presented itself to her mind, yet she shrank from it—shrank from pouring her tale into that woman's ears. Why was it? She had no reason whatever. It was one of those inexplicable instincts which seize upon the mind. Therefore she consumed her grief in silence and solitude. And Pierce, her father and her teacher—why not fly to him for advice and help in this the first misery of her young life? Because she would not blame Louis. Pierce would instantly come to the conclusion that it was Louis's fault. The feeling of the wife revolted against casting blame upon her husband; still greater was the dislike which arose after a time in her mind to reveal his lack of the qualities she had loved him for. No; it must remain a secret in her heart; she would show no sign. Heloise did not think all this out in strict reasoning, but it passed half unconsciously through her mind. So she became an almost total recluse, seldom leaving the mansion night or day. So he, too, became an almost total absentee ; never seen in the evening; coming home in the early hours of the morning, sleeping till noon, sitting by himself the afternoon, or passing out into the Unknown ; for when he went out, to her he passed into the Unknown. Her mind could not suggest his probable course in that great desert of London.

Gradually their habits became entirely estranged. He had his rooms apart from hers—unconnected in any way; so that he could come in or out utterly without her knowledge. He never inquired after her motions.

The days grew longer and longer to Heloise ; the evenings almost unbearable. She had ceased to use those affectionate caresses and endearments to retain him at her side. She recognised their utter powerlessness. Her step grew languid and slow; the old impetuousness and perpetual motion left her by degrees. The long evenings were her especial dread. It was thus that she recalled to mind, one night early in September, that they had been married just three months, only a quarter of a year. To her it seemed an age ago. That morning, when the joy bells rang out at Avonbourne, had faded away into the far-off distance. She tried to recall her feelings on that day. It was a vision; the whole scene had vanished—the hopes had fled.

Can you blame her, can you sneer at her? The warm tears *would* force themselves into her eyes, and for the first time Heloise, burying her face on the cushion of the ottoman, lost her whole consciousness in bitter, bitter weeping.

CHAPTER V.

She was standing on the broad steps that lead up to the entrance of the British Museum. The afternoon sun of the autumn day shone yellow and lurid upon her tall and commanding figure, while her wealth of golden hair glittered in the rays. Her right hand was slightly uplifted, pointing at the edifice, and her face was turned somewhat over her shoulder to address a gentleman who followed immediately behind. She was a grand and noble creature, this Georgiana Knoyle, the banker's sister — tall as a goddess of the classic time, large limbed, moulded in a generous and full-developed manner by the great artist Nature. No miserable and wretched tight-laced stays had disfigured her waist. It would have been called large in these artificial times, when the fetishes of fashion are so devoutly worshipped. But where in all the superb statues of antiquity will you find one single woman, meant to represent an ideal of beauty, with a small and wasp-like waist? The Venus de Medicis, all the statues of Venus, even the very Psyche— the ideal of fragility—one and all are sculptured with a torso, lessening in diameter, it is true, above the hips, but only gradually and gently so. The curve is slow and gradual; there is no sharp 'dig' inwards, so to say. The waist of the Venus, if a person of the same size were clothed in modern dress, would be called coarse and vulgar in this modern day. Yet the whole world has agreed to regard these statues as the canon of female beauty. Georgiana's shoulders, too, were called high and masculine by her friends—in good truth, they were perfectly developed, nothing more. They did not slope rapidly from her neck downwards, like the sides of a pyramid; they had a perceptible width, a breadth about them; in other words, she had a *chest*, which is what few women have, and in that chest was a pair of vigorous lungs and a regularly-beating healthy heart. Falser taste there cannot be than the artificial and acquired one which delights in a neck sloping like the eaves of a house, with prominent bust, no chest, small waist, and large hips. Falser still the miserable, affected, stilted walk which has been the rule of late years, as if all ladies suffered from weakness of the spine, and had an iron up it to keep the back at a certain angle with the legs, much as children's legs are sometimes ironed for weak ankles. The huge and extended 'bustle'—horrid excrescence!—found no place in Georgiana's dress. She walked perfectly upright, as God had designed her to walk, putting her feet firmly down upon the ground, feet unencumbered with narrow and high heels. Her limbs moved freely; hence her walk was striking and stately, as those antique statues would have walked could they have been warmed into life. Her dearest female friends called her high shouldered, large waisted, gawky; 'no figure, you know, my dear, but a very estimable person,

very, only somewhat eccentric.' In that peculiar hazy light, so soft and yet so lurid, her
face, turned towards him, and sculptured in
classic shape, with its clear and regular features, shone to him almost as that of a goddess, or of a Genius at least—the very Genius
of that place they were about to enter.

Commonplace British Museum, 'open to
the public every day except'—what day is it?
—'no refreshments allowed,' with its crowd
of commonplace people ; in Bloomsbury, poor,
paltry, and second-class Bloomsbury. A goddess here, a romance here, a Genius of this
place ? Pooh!

But a goddess and a Genius she seemed
to him, a noble and inspired creature, as she
paused a moment on those broad steps, and
a light shone out from her large gray eyes.

'This is the Temple, Neville,' she said in
a low voice, for there were others about, ' the
true and real sanctified place of worship, at
least of reverence. In these walls are collected
the fruit of man's inspirations and achieve-
ments, and the records of his thought, his

mind, his soul, for full six thousand years. What were the contents of the Delphic fane to the treasures that are here? What were the wretched gold and silver shields, the trophies, the offerings of kings and principalities—poor articles of uselessness stored up at Delphi—compared with the accumulated wisdom of ages carefully preserved here? The very Tabernacle itself, ay, and the temple of Solomon at Jerusalem, did not contain one-half the glory that lies hidden here. The spirit of God that dwelt with the prophets and the patriarchs, that inspired the founder of the Buddhist religion, of the Sabæan, of the Egyptian, of the Olympian—all these, and many more — is here. Here are the Bibles of the universe—not only the truths collected by one race, be they Hebrew, or Egyptian, or Hindoo, or Arabian, or Chinese, but the truths discovered by the souls of the mighty men, the chosen of Heaven, who have lived in all countries since the world began. And who, reading these in a proper and appreciative frame of mind, shall not feel the spirit of God, the Shechinah as it were, dwelling in this place? This is the Temple; this is the true consecrated spot. To me, Neville, it is grander far than the pretentious St. Paul's, grander than the St. Peter's at Rome. He who would find truth, let him come here.'

'I agree with you partly,' said Neville, as they passed on into the Museum. 'I think that it is a temple in the truest and most real meaning of the word; but to me the spirit, the divine inflatus, the Shechinah, never has dwelt or can dwell in any building or place which has been constructed by man. There is a something, an invisible influence, irradiating from the hewn stone, the mortar, which repels my mind—forces it back upon itself.

> "There, on the benches, in the hall,
> Thought, hearing, sight, forsake me all."

I cannot step, as it were, upon the tripod, and feel the divine spirit animating me in any spot where the mark of man's hand remains. It is an instinct, Georgie; I cannot help it. I recoil from the stone wall, the *hewn* stone.

It is an instinct deep down in the human soul; else how is it that the ancient worshipper built his altar of unhewn stone, and the Founder of the religion of our day ever lived, and spoke, and taught in the mountain, and the grove and the garden, surrounded by the works of His Father, not by the works of man's hands?   Beneath the shadow if only of a single tree, gazing dreamily upwards through the boughs and leaves at the azure sky, listening to the breeze—" the sound of a going in the tree-tops"—there is a something that enters into me, and carries me away with it in lofty dreams and hopes. Here there is none of that.   The inspiration here is of pure intellect only.'

' Perhaps it is the difference between our woman's and man's nature,' said Georgie; ' but I can think so much better and feel so much more *indoors*.   Outdoors I am distracted with so many things; so many trifles disturb me; my gaze rambles and my mind wanders. I require walls round me to shut it in.   These are the cases we came to see.'

Either for her blessing or for her curse Georgiana Knoyle had been gifted with a mind ample and vigorous beyond the usual allowance of her sex ; not that exactly, for it implies a want of mind in the majority ; but, in other words, she had a mind which, for a feminine one, was strongly scientific, logical, and masculine. Her brother, the banker, was conspicuous for the power and breadth of his intellect; but it had taken a different course. He had bent it upon money, and the result was evident in the enormous wealth which flowed at his feet. Her parents were long deceased, and left to herself entirely without trammels—for she had a competent fortune, and her brother never interfered—she developed a strongly-marked character. She was, in fact, an advocate of the mental and moral rights of women—not confining her conception of those rights to the power to sit in Parliament, or to vote, but looking rather to the æsthetic side of the question, arguing that women should receive a higher education, should be placed on a broader and freer platform. She did not attempt to prove that woman was equal, or ever could be equal, to man in strength, bodily or mental; what she did most earnestly believe and most earnestly advocate was, that, in her own particular way, woman had gifts parallel in utility to those of man. Woman should not strive to emulate or to mix indiscriminately with man. Her platform should be distinct, but equally high, and equally free and open. Strictly logical in all her deductions, reflective and contemplative to a superior degree, Georgiana recognised what no other leader of her party had done—that to place woman in such a position as this, to admit that such was the position she should occupy, was to reopen all those questions which the world had settled in effect, if not in detail, during the last six thousand years. She boldly admitted that the whole accepted theories of social government, and consequently of religion, must be reconstructed. They must be traced back to their original beginnings, and rebuilt up. In carrying out this idea to its conclusions, she saw that the very first commencement of such a scheme must be the rewriting (to coin a phrase) of history. The history of man must be rewritten. His real, and not his mythical, origin must be ascertained ; so that his relations with other men, and with Nature and Nature's laws, might be fully understood. That his history was at best but very imperfectly understood or suspected, Georgiana most fully believed. She saw that even in comparatively recent and well-recorded times vast populations, inhabiting whole continents of the earth, had lived out their natural lives and passed away without a monument, almost without a name. What had become of the enormous multitudes who had existed in the interior of Asia, and about whom we absolutely had nothing but faint traditions ? While the deeds, the wars, and policies of a single small state—a mere fraction of the human race— had been so vividly described by its historians, while Greece lived in the pages of Thucydides, Xenophon, and Herodotus, what had become of the huge hordes, the mighty

millions of unknown men, contemporaneous
with these events, but who were utterly lost
to sight?   Of the existence of such millions
the roll-call of Xerxes' army was a sufficient
proof.   But before these—before the dawn of
any written history, before the dawn even of
mythical history—what myriads of nations
must have lived and passed away without a
sign !   Before these again, in the glacial
period, in the pre-glacial period, according
to modern science, men had existed.   What
was their history?   What were their social
relations?   How did they stand in relation
to Nature and Nature's laws?   They had some
inkling of civilisation, it was clear; they had
weapons, tools, houses, tombs.   But before
them ?   The primeval inhabitants of earth,
who were they, and what was their history?
Were they an indescribable race—higher than
an ape and lower than a negro; half-breeds
between brute and human intelligence; or
were they as demi-gods, and were the existing races but deteriorating descendants of
these wondrous beings?

She saw that it was not her calling to go forth to the world, to stand upon the public platform or the week-day pulpit, preaching the masses into the conception of the idea of woman's equality. She was not gifted with the ready flow of speech, the quick repartee, necessary to such a career ; neither had she the peculiar strength of fibre, the calibre, for such battling hand to hand. Hers was the thoughtful part—her portion was the student's. Therefore she had addressed herself to this— to search out and discover the first beginnings of man upon the earth, to trace his history and his development, to write his prehistoric history. This was why she was examining the cases of prehistoric weapons in the Museum.

Neville did not agree with her in all things, accepted lover as he was, thoughtful and just to all who differed from him as he was. But on this one point their diverging theories met and held common course. Above all things it was necessary to search into the early history of man. Upon this must be

based the premisses from which a new, and
yet an old, faith and belief and social super-
structure must be reared. For he, too, was
reconstructing in his own mind, with deep
thought and reverent search for truth, that
fabric of belief which is necessary for the
repose of the human soul, and which science
had shattered to pieces.

Hence he threw himself with ardour into
her study, and laboured hard to furnish her
with new facts and new conjectures for her
projected work on the ' Prehistoric History
of Man.' He had been with her to Brussels,
to Vienna, to Paris, to a dozen other places
where the learned and the curious had preserved fragments of the great wreck of Time.
They were only lovers, yet he had accompanied her. In any other than Georgie the
scandal would have been great; but even the
gossip-loving coteries of highest and most
'particular' society could not even think of
wrong in connection with Georgiana Knoyle.
They laughed at her, sneered at her, but
secretly they acknowledged her depth and

strength of character. And these two had travelled in the most open manner : she with her
maids, and even footmen; he with his attend-
ants; never living at the same hotels; scru-
pulously observing the requirements of the
strictest propriety. The banker her brother
did not interfere; he spoke of it openly before all. Still, of course, society would have
cavilled, had it not been for her intense individuality, which overcame the breath of slan-
der. They knew that evil was impossible to
her; her intellect would forbid it. Temptation
even would never enter in at those calm serene
gray eyes. Moreover, there were many who
in their secret hearts, although they pro-
fessedly sneered at such things, yet gladly
hailed the innovation as one step in advance
in casting off those trammels which bound
women down like slaves—slaves of the drawing-room.

They were very happy, these two—Neville
and Georgie. He was a tall and noble-looking
man. That was not it; they were in such
perfect accord of soul. Though their creeds

differed in detail, yet they were working out the same great problems of existence.

This afternoon they were particularly interested in the large flint spear-head exhibited in one of these cases. Dating from an unknown antiquity, it showed a beauty of execution which seemed impossible in that rude age, in that rude material—so true its edge, so elegant its shape! It was wonderful how so hard and yet so splintery a substance as flint could be worked, without the aid of modern tools, to such perfection of form. But in these flints—which could tell no tales, which bore no inscriptions—Georgiana lamented that they seemed to have reached the limit of human research. The fragmentary record broke off with these, and before that all was darkness and obscurity.

Neville thought differently. He believed that vast fields of research were as yet unexplored. Lyell and other eminent geologists had demonstrated that the surface of the earth had been raised, and again lowered, and raised again; so that whole continents once teeming with population had been buried by degrees below the waves; and this ages before history began. The first thing to do was to decide the probable position and boundaries of these continents and countries of a prehistoric time. Then, with the aid of modern appliances, the whole area at the bottom of the sea should be trawled, which would bring up any surface remains of antique civilisation.

In all human probability the immobility of the water at such great depths had preserved the remains of man's works in as perfect a state as the pure air of Egypt had preserved the temples of that land. The diving-bell, too, at the present was a rude instrument; in the future it might be so improved as to allow of extended operations under water; and then, in interesting localities, excavations might be made, just as they are on earth, in the tumuli of the watery plains.

'But,' said Neville, 'what, above all other things, has always filled my mind with a species of fascination is the thought of the unknown regions that may lie stretching in vast sublimity of solitude in the extreme South. The Northern Pole is commonplace in comparison—it has been *surrounded* by man, the edge has been visited; but the South is a mystery. There the ice rises in one immense wall or cliff of two hundred feet in height, and this vast mountain of ice is but the edge of an illimitable glacier, slowly moving with the sea from countries utterly unvisited even in the myths of man. They tell us of the men of the glacier period— the progenitors, the aborigines of the known earth; may it not be possible that the remnants of that race, retiring with the retiring snow, may have followed the icy plains back into those remote regions, as the ancient Britons fell back before the invaders into Wales?'

'O Neville,' said Georgie, as they stood again on the steps of the Museum, on their way out, 'I had forgotten. I am ashamed. I have never visited my new sister!'

'Your new sister?'

'I mean Horton's wife's sister, then—
Louis's wife, Heloise. I have never seen her;
they say she is lovely. We came back from
Paris a week ago—she must think it very
strange of me. I will go immediately.'

Neville saw her to her carriage, and hail-
ing a hansom himself, drove to his chambers.

CHAPTER VI.

He knew that Knoyle was the name of his mistress's sister; he knew they were family relations. He knew that his mistress was always in the second drawing-room that overlooked the garden in the evening. Thus it was that the footman committed the greatest mistake he had ever made in his life. Without first seeing that his mistress was ready to receive, he ushered Georgiana straight into the room, where Heloise was lying on the ottoman. Hearing footsteps she started up, and her tear-stained face and disordered hair gave Georgie a shock. She felt, too, that she had intruded; but it was too late to go back. She walked rapidly to Heloise, and took both her hands, and kissed her.

It is impossible to recount in hard dry words, in expressionless ink, how this grand and noble woman soothed the throbbing heart of poor Heloise, and by slow steps strengthened her to meet her misery with greater firmness. Before that one evening was past all had been confided to Georgie. Instinctively Heloise felt that she had found a friend on whose arm she might lean, to whom she might cling, as it was necessary to her fragile nature to cling to some one. And Georgie found here a mission, it may be more truly glorious, if not so high sounding, as the search for prehistoric history.

From that evening the visits of Georgiana became more and more frequent, until at last not a day passed without her presence; and she grew to be a part of Heloise's daily life. There was something about Heloise which was singularly attractive to one of Georgie's temperament. She was so unaffected—so purely natural, without any of the *blasé* air so common to those who have moved much in society. Her heart was open. Georgie soon found the way to it. Here, too, was a new field for her mission. Here was a rare opportunity to put into practice that work which she had in view. Very slowly, and by imperceptible degrees, Georgie drew Heloise's mind to dwell upon the destiny and the position of woman in the abstract. This in itself was a relief to Heloise's overburdened mind, strained and tired with too much brooding upon herself. And it was so entirely novel. The very idea of attempting to alter the social relations of woman had never been presented to her before. She had never questioned the present state of things ; never doubted but that they were natural and right. The very naïveness of her questions and remarks often disconcerted Georgie; but she persevered, and in time had so far succeeded, that Heloise really did of her own will look around her, and begin to compare the condition of woman as she was with the condition of woman as she might be.

But here arose a danger which Georgie had not foreseen, but of which she afterwards blamed herself as the originator and cause. Heloise, from the consideration of the rights and wrongs of woman in the abstract, by a very simple process of reasoning began to reflect upon the possibility of an improvement in her own position. Was her contract of marriage with Louis the right or the wrong thing? Was it a holy and perpetual bond, as she had been taught to believe, or was it a tyranny and an unjust repression of her nature?

Questioning herself in this way, Heloise, after a while, came to ask herself, did she love this man Louis? The question occurred to her as it were suddenly, and as a shock. It made her tremble a little, as she thought of it. It made her feel guilty. She was ashamed of herself—she felt so unfaithful to him. She drove the idea out of her mind—for the time at least.

Louis was less and less at home. But he was quite aware of the growing intimacy between his wife and Georgiana Knoyle, and he knew, too, the nature of the teaching which Georgie was striving to inculcate. When he was at home he would come and sit with them, and sneer at her in his Mephisto-like manner. He did not repeat the old jibes of woman's incompetency, but he thrust in sharp observations of his own completely new to Georgie. They silenced her for the moment; but the very fact of an opposition was enough to rouse her zeal, and she studied and searched her authorities to discover a reply. Then he treated her with contemptuous indifference.

Though she tried to be more than woman, Georgie could not suppress a rising hatred of this man, which she called to herself indignation at his treatment of Heloise, but which arose quite as much from her own wounded self-esteem. Thus it came about that she grew to some extent interested in his goings out and movements. She watched him after a manner. It was easy to track him, for his steps led always to one place; and the beaten path was clear to follow, though Heloise, in her simplicity, had never suspected it. He was always at Carlotta's. The great banker was at Berlin, or rather he vibrated between Berlin and Paris, engaged in momentous matters of statecraft and money commingled;

but his peeress remained at her mansion in the West-end, notwithstanding the fact that the season was long over. Louis was there for ever. He did not attend upon Carlotta in public; but her house was rarely ever free of him.

Georgie soon learnt this. Her heart—her untamable woman's heart — began to burn fiercely with rage and hatred of Louis, and mingled with it was no small share of dislike of Carlotta, between whom and herself there had never been the slightest approach to familiarity. The peeress looked down with ineffable contempt, from the height of her own sublime elevation, her aristocratic position, her unquestioned and striking beauty, upon that poor 'eccentric creature with the enormous waist.' . Georgie felt that Carlotta despised her, and although she professed and tried hard not to care a rap, it was impossible to utterly subvert the workings of her heart. She never would have admitted to herself that she hated Carlotta, but such in fact was the case.

Under the pretext, then, that it was in the

interest of Heloise, she became an earnest observer of what took place ' between Louis and Carlotta. She began to debate in her own mind the propriety of remonstrating with her brother, and calling his attention to the super-abundant familiarity, the rather too great intercourse which existed between his wife and Louis. She seriously contemplated a journey to Berlin, to open his eyes, to disabuse him of that fatuous and blind belief in his wife, the peeress, which he appeared to have. But Georgie was, be it remembered, a sharp and logical reasoner. How would Horton receive her? Would he not, in his calmly practical way, point out to her that she had over-stepped even the bounds of sisterly affection in thus coming between a man and his wife? He would assuredly ask her for proofs; and where were her proofs? Proofs of what? She was obliged to own to herself that she did not even know what it was she required proof of. Louis's simple visits went for nothing. And a little self-condemnation arose in her mind as she remembered that she herself had not always acted on the strict lines of decorum and propriety, as laid down by the world. Her ramblings from one capital to another in company with Neville were much more suspicious, looked at in this light, than the mere visits of Louis, especially to a mansion full of servants, full of eyes and ears ever on the watch. No; she dared not go to Horton. Thinking it over still more deeply, Georgie became convinced that, whatever amount of badinage or even strong flirtation there might be, there was nothing worse between Louis and Carlotta. She was forced, in spite of herself, to do this much justice to her sister-in-law. She remembered Carlotta's career; her imperious manner; her overweening vanity and self-reliance; her almost fierce self-assertion; the potential force of her individuality. A mind and soul so wholly given up to vanity and to ambition was of necessity armour-proof against all dangerous affections. It was a relief to her mind to feel that, whatever Carlotta might do, she was perfectly pure.

That there was something—that there was

a secret undercurrent of something[1]—was obvious from one single fact alone: Carlotta never came to visit Heloise. Regularly twice a week her carriage called, and a polite inquiry was made; but never by any chance did she call or invite Heloise to her own house. There was a tacit suspension of relationship.

Heloise was calmer, even in a sense happy, with Georgie; but she did not recover her old impetuous manner. The lightness, the spring and elasticity, had gone from her movements; the flash had left her eye. She lived in a subdued manner; her vivacity was absent.

These circumstances of real life, so different from any which she had as yet encountered, brought home the difficulties of her theory vividly to Georgie's mind: how to arrange the social relations so as to amend and ameliorate these jars and discords; how provide against their recurrence under any new system. And as Heloise had done, so Georgie in her turn began to contemplate the position in which she herself stood with regard to the new creed of the rights and wrongs of woman. She was engaged to Neville; the marriage was rapidly approaching. At such a time, when her feelings were naturally peculiarly sensitive, the spectacle of these two unhappy marriages came before her eyes. She had heard of such things before. But now the whole details of the thing were laid bare to her eyes with a trying minuteness. It was true that Neville, as she recollected with a glow of natural satisfaction, was not like either of those men, Horton or Louis. It was also true—ah, Georgie, your vanity peeped out there—that she herself was different. But there were indefinite possibilities of discord evidently in married life. And what struck her as the worst of all was the impossibility of escape when once the ceremony was completed. Let the wife be never so miserable, let the husband be never so disagreeable, there was no escape. It was only after the close intercourse which followed marriage that the true characteristics of man and woman came out; it was in that familiar relation that the weak points first came into view.

Louis had sneeringly said the other day that wives, in his opinion, ought to have written characters, as servants had; and if the character was false or overdrawn, the husband should have the power to dissolve the marriage, and to prosecute the parent or guardian who had given him a wrong estimate of his bride. Georgie had bitterly retorted, that if the bride should be furnished with a written character, the bridegroom should be required to furnish two sureties in large sums for his good behaviour.

Georgie, with a smattering of physiology, had heard that the human being, at the end of three or seven years, at all events after a certain period of time, became totally re-organised. Every atom of the body was supplanted by another atom, new and strange. How, then, could a person, after this period of time, when this great and organic change had taken place, be supposed to retain the old affections in their full entirety? After three or seven years Neville might cease to love her. To look at the wretched state of things around her, one would think that this organic change in some people took place much more rapidly. Heloise had barely been married four months.

Much as she loved him, Georgie began to doubt and to hesitate greatly to take the final and irrevocable vows with Neville.

CHAPTER VII.

Extreme ease and elegance of manner—an *abandon* the result of the highest breeding —curiously contrasted with an evident, and therefore vulgar, satisfaction with the flavour of a prime cigar. How inimitable the saunter; how Olympian the lounge! Ages of natural selection must have passed away before the survival of the fittest finally led to the production of so perfect a specimen of idleness. He was a very handsome fellow—there were no two opinions about that—and it was clear enough that he knew it. There was a delicious complacency about him, as much as to say that the whole world was contained within the compass of his waistcoat. If all within that waistcoat was happy and at peace, the universe must necessarily be in the highest possible state of beatitude. Holding the cigar between the tips of two white and slender fingers of the left hand—fingers glittering with rings—he held it at a little distance from his lip, and the smoke rose up from the ash in graceful curls over his shoulder, while at the same time he cast sidelong glances at his figure reflected in the plate-glass windows of Regent-street. The wrists of a pair of lavender-kid gloves just protruded far enough to be seen from the bosom of his waistcoat—a bosom displaying a breadth of snow-white linen, with diamond studs flashing in the sunlight. A heavy gold chain passed across, and as it were braced, his figure, which diminished so elegantly at the waist as to give rise to the suspicion of the agency of stays. But that could hardly be: no stays could ever allow that peculiar swaying easy motion, obviously free from the least restraint. The suit—ah, the suit!—was indescribable. There was an air about it—the beauty of perfect proportion. His right hand carried a light cane, which he was perpetually swinging and holding in various positions, so as to fully display the dazzling whiteness of the small hand, and to flash the diamond ring on the finger. Down to the very boots the same overweening vanity exhibited itself. They were certainly very small feet, and very perfectly proportioned, and the instep was high and haughty; and not one of these advantages was hidden. This man was not one of those who hide their light under a bushel. A very dainty individual indeed! Notwithstanding the extreme affectation of the man, the most disgusted observer must have admitted that he was singularly handsome. The hawk-like eye —so large and full and dark, and burning with suppressed fire—was in itself a feature which no one could pass by without noticing. The nose was straight and delicately sculptured—hardly long enough or decided enough for a man, but exquisite in its carving. Long dark eyelashes swept the cheek, and a wealth of blue-black ringlets clustered round the ears and back of the head. These ringlets had been allowed to grow to a length almost too great for a gentleman in our stiff modern time, but the solecism might be excused in even a man with such beautiful hair. But the lips were the loveliest part of him—so large and yet so delicately scarlet, and curved like the bow of the god of love—sensuous warm lips, that looked as if they fed on the dew of maidens' kisses. A very Don-Juan-looking man—such a fellow as you didn't very often meet. There was one drawback even to all this elegance and beauty. There is always a defect in all things mortal. Nothing is ever absolutely perfect. Even in the Venus de Medicis critics have been heard to declare that one leg was a little longer than the other. He was a trifle too stout. There was an obvious inclination to stoutness, and some indication of an excessive rotundity below the waistcoat. But even this only added to the air of complete complacency—the sleepy repose of the whole being.

How daintily he sauntered over the clean pavement, as gingerly as if it had been the dirtiest road! With what a hypercritical air he glanced in at the shop-windows! He paused before the famous photographic shop, where all the notabilities of the hour are shown—from Bismarck and Don Carlos, or the Archbishop of Canterbury, to the latest ballet-dancers. Raising his eyeglass he superciliously examined the arm of that fair candidate for popular favour, and the leg of this. Easy enough to see upon what particular limb or feature the *artiste* depended to attract; it was always so prominently, so carefully displayed. Don Juan found fault with all; his gaze rested on neither long. This arm was too thick, too bulky at the shoulders; but then the public like size, something palpable and palpitating. This leg had too much calf, and that not enough; and O, what horrid hair! As for Bismarck and the Archbishop of Canterbury—pah! they were beneath notice. So we stroll on—lazily, softly, with our eyes half closed—taking no note of any passerby; seeing nothing, feeling nothing, conscious of nothing but our own dear, delicious, darling self. Only we pause—we slacken our idle pace—one moment by Rimmel's, that our nostrils may be refreshed with the odour of innumerable flowers, and our soul, smelling a 'sweet savour,' may be strengthened to proceed through this poor dusty London, graced for a brief hour with our presence.

It was the time when the toiling artisans of London had already lived half a day. Rising at six, working steadily till noon, they had already finished half a day, and covered with dust and grime, weary with labour, were about to snatch a short hour of repose. They were permitted as a favour to grind their hard cheese and drink their vulgar porter; or, if they could afford it, they might even swallow a reeking mutton-chop. You see, some of us are made of mud, and some of us are made of cream and sugar, of almond paste, like the rind of a wedding-cake.

Our darling knocked at a friend's at this particular hour, in order that he might enter and breakfast. Louis's chambers were exquisitely fitted up, particularly they were furnished with every appliance for lounging. This was *his* temple, which he had dedicated to himself. Heloise had never heard of these chambers; Louis never thought of them while he was in love (about three months); now he had recovered he found them extremely convenient. Here, without the slightest fear of interruption, he could indulge to the utmost in that cultivation of himself which was the very core and centre of his philosophy.

'My dear Charles,' said Louis, not troubling to rise from his couch, but extending the tip of his fingers, 'I had given you up, and had commenced my coffee.'

' My dear Charles' very leisurely deposited his hat on the top of a Sèvres vase, and without taking the slightest notice of his host, sat, or rather reposed, himself upon another couch; for Louis allowed no chairs in his establishment. The Romans, said he, were our masters in luxury. Their civilisation had none of that driving, hurrying, scurrying haste about it; none of that dustiness—no smoke and steam and shoeblacks. There was a graceful repose in their very hurry. It was all a state of *festina lente*. Even Julius Cæsar himself, who posted one hundred miles a day through pathless forests, over rivers and deserts, with such celerity as to anticipate intelligence of his movements, nevertheless found time, in the very moment of his death-agony, to fold his gown gracefully around his falling figure. There was a finish, a supreme polish, about these classical people which he, Louis, peculiarly admired. They carried it into the very smallest matters. What, for instance, less worthy of thought and care than the very dirt —the common earth—under a house? But these Romans—these artists—extended their care to the minutest trifles. This was how they prepared the foundation of a house or the floor of their halls : firstly, the damp earth was all carefully removed to the depth of several feet; then a layer of stones, rubble, and rough pieces of broken tile was placed as a groundwork. Over this was spread a layer of charcoal a few inches thick; over this a layer of finer gravel, and a fourth of hardest cement, on which the mosaic pavement was superposed. What careful provision against damp feet! What finished beauty in the meanest matters! These men — who were men, not ciphers who had to hasten hither and thither as mere parts of some huge sum in figures—never sat on chairs; except, indeed, their magistrates when on duty. A chair was something so hard and angular, so upright and stiff. They reclined with graceful ease upon couches and pillows. Thus they added to the zest and pleasure of eating the charming sensation of repose. Louis, following this example, rigidly excluded all chairs, and all furniture approaching to the definition of a chair, even a footstool, from his rooms. Couches constructed from sketches of his own surrounded a table upon three sides. These couches were not flat, like the ordinary sofa, but the bed of the couch rose gradually like an inclined plane; and thus the body of the reposing person was prevented from feeling that disagreeable sense of repletion which must accompany eating in a lying position. The fourth side of the table was open to allow of the approach of the attendant, who thus placed the dish or the plate at once before you, without leaning over your shoulder or shoving it edgewise in at your side. But Louis had added the conveniences of modern science to the elegances and comforts of ancient civilisation. By the side of each guest, in a small depression in the table, was a tiny ivory knob, the slightest pressure upon which instantly summoned an obedient slave by means of the electric flash. Each of the four corners of the room was hung with heavy purple curtains, leaving only a small space of the wall visible; and these small spaces, or panels, were painted, as at Pompeii, with *poses* of the nude figure, much as were Horace's chambers, according to that scurrilous and libellous Suetonius. Louis's defence of these sensuous and luscious pictures was ingenious and philosophical. He argued that something of such pleasure was essential, and indeed necessary, to the existence of mankind. If, therefore, they were necessary, it was better to enjoy them in this æsthetic and artistic way than through the mediation of the ruder and more primeval instincts.

There is nothing so difficult to furnish as a breakfast-table. Of course it is easy enough for your lean and toiling rustic, whose rasher of greasy bacon and hunch of bread pleases his ravenous appetite. There are those who are content with potted salmon or even kippered herrings!

But your true epicure—your noonday riser—finds it extremely difficult to discover new and charming delicacies for his breakfast-table. It is easy comparatively to order a dinner. There is a breadth, a largeness, about dinner which affords ample room for the display of genius. The very succession of courses gives a scope which the one single spread of breakfast can never allow. Dinner is like a three-volume novel; breakfast is like an epigram. In the one you may be diffusive; in the other you must be pointed, or you are nowhere. Alas, how many suffering individuals, to whom Heaven has not vouchsafed an idea, have to be content with soda-water and brandy for their 'matins'! But Louis's breakfast-table was perfection—ever varied, ever delicate and appetising.

'My dear Charles' appreciated it greatly.

He ate, he drank, he sipped, he tasted, **and**
said nothing; but his silence was more appreciative than words. One could imagine now
how that rotundity under the waistcoat came
into existence. People pay to see the lions
fed; how much more to watch the gods at their
meals! The cigar had not dulled the palate.
Then he leant back and sighed gently, closed
his eyes, and tapped slowly and musically with
a silver spoon upon the table.

'My dear Charles,' said Louis, in a voice
of winning entreaty, soft and low; and extending one hand he began to play with the wealth
of black ringlets. Charles opened his eyes
with a flash which made the other draw back
as if he had seen lightning. Then Louis
drew nearer, and began to purr. This old
serpent of five-and-thirty had a low melo-
dious voice (when he chose so to pitch it),
and his words, rolling out softly and sweetly,
filled the room with a monotonous cadence,
like the murmur of falling waters—soft, endearing words—till Charles closed his eyes
again. The spoon ceased to rap; Charles was

asleep. Then Louis fingered the ringlets, and admired the long and drooping eyelashes, and kissed the delicate white hand, and Heaven knows where his caresses might have wandered, only Charles, starting up, dealt him a blow which flung him back, showing that that shapely shoulder had much muscularity.

'Carlotta!' hissed Louis, in a temper.

'Idiot!' replied the peeress, showing her brilliant teeth; for it was the banker's consort. Why did he go trout-fishing to rest his mind?

'I'll stand no more of it,' said Louis, frowning.

Carlotta hummed the end of a favourite opera tune, beating time with her forefinger in the air like a leader of a band.

> ' " Such is your old coquette, who can't say No
> And won't say Yes, and keeps you in an offing
> On a lee shore till it begins to blow—
> Then sees your heart wreck'd with an inward scoffing." '

Not that Louis had much of a heart; but

he had a little feeling, and she had just been demolishing his exquisite breakfast, for the preparation of which he deserved some trifling reward.

.‘ It’s that fellow Noel,’ sneered Louis.

‘ Yes, it’s that fellow Noel,’ smiled Carlotta.

‘ I’ll kick his—’

‘ No, you won’t.’

‘ With a face like brickdust, two teeth gone, a slit nose, and a hole in his ear !’

‘ *Mon brave!*’

‘ D—n !’

Silence, save the peeress’s low hum. Suddenly she started, picked up her hat and cane.

‘ Send me round this vase,’ she said, pointing to the one on which her hat had hung.

‘ I sha’n’t,’ said Louis snappishly, like a child deprived of its plaything.

There was a sound of a smash, and the fragments flew about the room. Carlotta had sent her cane through it.

‘Ta-ta!’

‘ I’ll never speak to you again.’

‘O yes, my dear, you’ll be round in the evening.’

She was gone. Louis, listening to her boots upon the stairs, swore to himself that she was right; he should be there in the evening, quarrel as they might. As for Noel, he reflected that Carlotta could never find a man she would trust like him. He smiled as he thought of this; she would never dare it with another. How came she, then, to dare it with him? The thought filled him with inexpressible satisfaction. The high and haughty peeress, the woman of the world, had descended to this for him! It filled him with a sense of his own personal charms. He lit a cigar. He had not forgotten Noel, nor forgiven Carlotta her flirtation with that battered warrior; but a feeling had arisen in his mind that he was quite capable of dealing with them both, and it would go hard if he could not turn this very detestable Noel to some purpose of utility in the end.

CHAPTER VIII.

IF you want to feel yourself a unit, a poor, solitary, wandering iota of humanity, to realise your impotent individuality, go to one of those enormous hotels which grace, or disgrace, the termini of the chief railways in London. There is a crowd on the platform, and you are nobody very particular amongst them; but that is distinction itself compared to what will follow a daring plunge into the wilderness waiting to swallow you up. The hurrying crowd of travellers, busied in getting tickets, labelling their luggage (when will the nuisance of luggage be abated?), discussing the probable time of starting, and driving the guards wild with reiterated questions,—all these are too much occupied to notice *you*. Whether your necktie be a hair's breadth too much on one side, or accurately placed with compass and ruler, matters very little. No one notices; none think of anything but themselves. But there is a certain feeling of a common humanity; a degree of common interest makes the crowd akin. One is not quite alone here. Open those great glass doors and once pass within, and you are absolutely, incontrovertibly 'nobody.' Instead of 'Railway Hotel,' they should write over them, 'Yourselves abandon, ye who enter here.' Two grand porters in scarlet and black, with lace upon their coats, approach you in state, and inquire if there is any luggage. If the reply is no, you instantly fall fifty per cent in their estimation. No gentleman could possibly travel without luggage; only a rambling idiot, only a fellow who makes a convenience of our hotel for one night, a mere nobody. They fall back disgusted, and a gentleman clad in the highest perfection of the tailor's art, whom you take to be at least the Austrian ambassador staying here a day or two, and to whom you involuntarily bow, glides up and asks, with a

slightly foreign accent, if you would like to
see your room, to dress before dinner? Or
would you like to go to the coffee-room, or
any of the public rooms? (accent again.) You
feel that if you say the coffee-room or the
smoking-room, you will be looked down upon
as still more a nobody; so you say, 'My room,
certainly,' with as grand an air as you can
manage, though what on earth you have to
do when you get to it you can't conceive.
The gentleman then makes out a ticket, on
which your name and address are entered,
and with a graceful wave of the hand directs
you towards an iron door.   In amazement,
not unmixed with terror, you behold an
octagon-shaped chamber, lighted up within,
through the bars of this iron door.   In the
moment you pause you observe that the iron-
work is curiously carved or hammered out in
a mediæval design, which word carries you
back to the days of torture and dungeons,
and you fancy you behold the dungeon.
There is a man in uniform within, who holds
a rope in one hand, and glares at you malig-

nantly.   This is, no doubt, the executioner.
But the door swings open, some extraordinary gibberish issues from the lips of your gen-
tleman-waiter, and you step in, in very dread
lest he should see you were a mere parvenu,
and unused to this sort of thing.   In an instant the floor rises up beneath you like the
deck of a ship at sea, the iron door passes
out of sight, and nothing remains but the man
who pulls hard at the rope.   Before you can
speak another iron door appears, and behind
there stands a woman, say rather a lady,
smartly dressed.   The door opens, you step
out; the executioner brands you in a loud voice
as 'No. 70, Floor Three,' and you feel a con-
victed felon on the way to your cell.   The
lady marches before, and you follow, shrinking every moment into a meaner wretch. The
corridor is broad enough to admit the whole
of your house, and nearly high enough, and
the floor is carpeted with what you take to
be red velvet.   Glancing back you see it ex-
tends into the illimitable distance—empty,
vast, noiseless.   There is not a soul but you—

only in the extremest dimmest distance there flit to and fro a few vague shadowy figures. After walking a quarter of a mile a door is opened, your lady lights your gas, and this is your room. It is as large as your dining-room, and rather more lofty. The bedstead of brass is hung with magnificent crimson curtains; the furniture is solid oak, plain oak; the very footstool is large, grand, covered with red velvet. Reverently you look round, and know not where to sit, or indeed what to do with yourself. After a while, in the belief that it is incumbent upon you to do something, you feebly take out your Brad-shaw and place it on the mantelpiece, as a sign that you are in possession. Then you sit down and gaze vacantly at the paper on the walls, and wait till you think you have 'seen your room' long enough—it is important not to commit a solecism. Next comes the search for the coffee-room. You debate whether you had better ring the bell and ask the chamber-maid the way, or whether it will be more *au fait* to walk boldly out and venture, as Ulysses

did, out into the waste, not of water, but of
carpet:

> ' It may be we shall find the happy Isles,
> And see the great Achilles whom we knew.'

Very gently you open the door and peep
like a criminal down the gallery—an ocean of
unending space. No, you will ring the bell
—but where is it? Evidently there is no
bell. So at last out you venture, and after
rambling hither and thither in this silent and
enormous hall, and passing two or three
waiters, who take not the slightest notice of
you, you at last run right against your 'lady,'
and have to ask her the way. 'Why did you
not ring, sir?' 'There was no bell.' 'O yes,
sir, there is—by the bed. Press on the knob.'
In a crushed state, miserable, wretched, feeling like a grain of sand under the base of the
Pyramid, you crawl down three flights of
stairs, swallow your coffee in a melancholy
mood, and go to bed at ten. Sure enough there
is the ivory knob by the bed-head—an electric
bell. But you console yourself that you will

sleep well—the bed at least is as clean and sweet as your own at home. In repose you will forget all. No. You doze off, it may be, an hour or two hours; you wake up in the belief that the last day has come, that the trump of the archangel has been blown, and all the thunders of heaven are let loose. You listen, awe-struck. Roar succeeds to roar, boom succeeds to boom — now dying away, now rising again, now sustained, never entirely gone—one long heavy roll of ceaseless artillery. Your heart beats violently, and you expect every moment to hear voices shouting 'Fire!' 'Murder!' 'Thieves!' or 'Earthquake!' But there is not a step, not a voice; nothing but boom, boom, boom, boom! You notice that a light comes in through the glass over your door; the gas then is gently burning in the gallery. This somewhat calms you. But again you think that an earthquake is taking place—that all the waiters have fled and left you to your fate; you will never get out of that labyrinth of passages. Fly! Make the attempt; stay not for trousers or

vest.   At last you remember that you are in
a railway hotel.   It must be the trains underneath ; the heavy luggage trains coming in
at night with meat and corn and coal and
stores. Gods, what trains too! What chop-
ped-up mountains they must be carrying to
make this enormous building vibrate as it
does! You listen till your ears ache with the
sound.   An insane desire comes over you to
rise and dress, and seek some quiet and small
private hotel, even some commercial establishment—anything away from this terrible
vastness, this void which crushes you, this
boom which rolls over you like huge waves.
At last, wearied out, you sleep.

What I was going to say when I began
this chapter was — Have hotels any conscience? This is not meant to refer either
to the price of the wines, or the fees to the
waiters, or even to the fleas, or the long bills.
Neither does it apply to railway hotels, which,
by the exigencies of their position, have no
means of knowing anything of their visitors,
for good or bad.

But there is such a thing as a Divorce Court; and whenever a case comes on of sufficient interest to be fully reported, the sin is always charged on the hotel. Captain So-and-so comes to such and such an hotel with somebody else's wife; and there they lived very comfortably, and nobody ever thought of anything wrong. Now have hotels any conscience? Why do they permit such things as these? why do they pander to vice? Surely after all the experience the people who keep them must have gained, they must be able to tell in a moment if anything is wrong. But up drive a gentleman and a lady, both well dressed, with plenty of luggage—that's the grand point; obviously they mean to stay, and obviously they have plenty of money. The lady may have a ring on, or she may not; or the chambermaid may note that the linen is marked with two different names, or what not. But here the reverse is true of the old proverb—this is the exception to Solomon's remark; the walls here have no ears. As the newspapers say, 'improper familiarities' took place at 'an hotel.' Conscience-stricken hotels, how they must wince at these exposures!

The fellow knew how to dine, at all events. The waiter saw that, and attended on him the more obsequiously. Moreover, he did not confine himself to one wine or two— he had the right wine at the right moment, and he only drank a glass or two of each. And she? She was very timid at first, and only trifled with her plate; but after a while the potent champagne, taken in ever such small quantities, rose up in the pretty little head, and then the eyes began to lift themselves to his face and to sparkle, and the conversation began—the which, of course, the waiter took good care not to hear, not he. Half-a-sovereign as a fee for serving at a dinner was not got every day; he would take precious good care nobody disturbed them! So he said to his sub. he would take good care nobody went in, unless specially rung for. O, the wickedness of the world!

There was nothing so very bad after all

in a young man of five-and-twenty treating a
full-blown lady—quite able to take care of
herself, as far as forty-five years went—to a
really good dinner. Only it was the incon-
gruity; highly incongruous—nothing more.

Virgil, in the *Bucolics* or *Georgics*, or
somewhere (it is vulgar to quote correctly),
has a beautiful description of the fierce and
passionate love that animated the horses which
lived in his days. The whole passage must
be read to be appreciated. There were times
when the very abundance of this tenderness
carried them to excesses.

Smothered fires must burst out somewhere
and at some time. A hayrick, if fired near
the ground, will smoulder for days before it
bursts into flame. Modern society supposes
the existence of thousands of human creatures
—fairly well fed, well dressed, moderately
handsome, or at least not positively bad looking—but who, having the misfortune to be
ladies, are supposed to have no feelings.
They have every appendage for the production of sensation, and every organ perfect—

they have eyes and nose and ears and hands, &c.—but they are supposed to have no feelings at all. Some of them keep schools, hundreds go out as governesses, hundreds dawdle about at home or with their relations. On the aggregate there must be some hundreds of thousands of them. Nobody will marry them ; they have no money. They are not superlatively good looking; most of them are well bred and educated, and have ladylike manners—but that counts for nothing. Fellows may admire, even love, but they will not marry. No fellow will marry except for money ; this they learn pretty speedily. No one boxes their ears physically ; but their ears, poor girls, are morally boxed all their lives—especially by their employers, their mistresses, and their richer relations who have to keep them. They are snubbed for ever; toned down; used as dummies to heighten the contrast ; trodden on. They have no feeling. They are made to bitterly understand the value of money by daily teaching of their own valuelessness. In the course of years all this reacts upon them, and they, too, resolve never to marry except for money. This is as it should be; the commercial spirit should be introduced into everything—into agriculture and matrimony. As they cannot marry, what are they to do? Do nothing, says modern society; feel nothing; be 0's— ciphers. No one will ever put a permanent unit against them.

This is all very well, and very proper and decorous. Only one thing is left out of sight and quite forgotten. This is Nature. Nature is of no account, 'tis true, nowadays; nobody ever thinks of Nature, or natural things or affections either, for the matter of that. The railways stretch all over the country, and bind Nature down in an iron web. The artificial laws of society stretch over the human heart and hold it down. There are dangerous appearances, though, sometimes of a certain amount of heaving and throbbing underneath. Some socialist physicians think the corset ought to be loosened a little. They talked of introducing a Bill into the House of Commons legalising marriage for a limited period, for three or four years, or seven, as the parties liked ; on the expiration of which time they might renew the lease—if they wished. They thought this would relieve the throbbing hearts that throb in vain.

But Exeter Hall! These three words are a paragraph in themselves. Nothing need be added to them.

As we said before, smouldering fires will burst out in the end. Now in all these thousands of female bosoms without feelings there must of necessity be one or two, just a berry or so on the topmost branch, who *do* possess feelings, and very fiery Cleopatra-like ones likewise. Screwed down, constrained, restrained, chained, bound up, trodden on, snubbed, still Maud, at five-and-forty, retained some little beauty of a kind, and still the smouldering fire in her burnt and smouldered. Poor wretch, what an existence hers had been! A galley slave's were preferable, for galley slaves can at least *swear*—which is a relief, though so awfully wicked. But a governess, compelled to spend fifty out of her sixty pounds per annum in dress to appear tolerably decent in a drawing-room, must not swear. Such had Maud been from her youth up. Poor wretch!

At last the fire burst out, as it was bound to do before she died, and all the worse, ay, ten times, a thousand times worse, for this quarter of a century of suppression. Her eyes had been opened to a safe way of enjoying mischief by her present mistress's nephew, Victor Knoyle, Esq. Nominally she was taking her holidays, with a distant relation far away on the western shores of Scotland. Really and truly she was dining at an hotel in the heart of London, not three miles from her employer's door, and with that employer's nephew. O, crime beyond forgiveness, unpardonable sin! Poor Maud! It was, perhaps, bad for you that Victor was somewhat of a genius. He had ideas; he had shown her one or two of these. He had made a discovery—somehow he managed to convey it to her. It was a safe way of indulging mischief.

So they drank the champagne, and laughed and talked and joked, and the world moved on around them, and London rushed and surged and roared unheard and unheeded. She was indulging in a little innocent masculine society *all to herself*—a thing for which she had parched and burnt for a quarter of a century. How many thousands are longing for the same thing at this hour! There is a lesson in this book, or rather there will be before the end is reached. But Exeter Hall!

Victor did not love her—she knew that; but he was *kind*. He did not cheat himself and his conscience by making himself believe that he loved her—she was too old. He had not the excuse of an all-absorbing love; but he felt an indescribable pleasure in placing food before this famished creature—for famished she was for a *little* love, a little tenderness. And it was quite safe; she would receive no harm; her reputation would remain intact. He had arranged to utilise his discovery if necessary.

They drank more champagne, and were very happy. It was such a relief to Maud. She sighed in the midst of her joy—a long-drawn sigh, as an invalid does when first taken out of the sick-chamber into the fresh air.

CHAPTER IX.

HORTON KNOYLE's brother Charles fell in love
with Carlotta at the same time that he did.
Carlotta chose Horton for several very good
reasons. Firstly, because Horton was richer
by far; secondly, because he had a fashionable and distinguished connection; thirdly,
because he was younger; and lastly, because
Charles had been previously married and was
a widower with two young sons. There was
no question, no thought at all, 'as to which
loved her most. It was a pro and con, a
debit and credit, account in her mind. Horton had the largest amount of credit. Charles
never ceased to love her, and when he died,
which he did about ten years ago, his will
was so ordered that in the event of his sons
dying without children, the property, some
95,000*l.*, went to Carlotta. Now Horton

was trustee and guardian to these young men, Victor and Francis, neither of whom could touch a penny of their fortune till they were twenty-five. Curiously enough he very carefully kept them out of the way and influence of their aunt Carlotta. One would have thought that a man busied with the affairs of nations would have been glad of a little assistance in training these charges; but no, he studiously secluded them from her. She was nothing loth, she had no desire to cumber herself with any concerns of theirs. So the two boys were sent to school, and finally to a private tutor's in a distant part of Sussex, where they remained. Horton would not allow them to go to college lest they should contract bad habits. He had no children of his own, and it seemed as if he was more than fidgety over these two boys, his nephews, and probably inheritors of his enormous wealth. Therefore they remained at the clergyman's in Sussex; strictly, carefully trained in the ways of virtue, and never so much as allowed to imagine the existence of vice. Even smoking, though not absolutely prohibited, was discouraged. They were required to be indoors at ten at latest. They were restricted to twenty pounds per quarter pocket-money; a mere nothing to young men from whom a knowledge of the wealth awaiting them some day could not be entirely concealed. Victor, the eldest, was turbulent and restless; Francis, the second, was milder and feebler, more easily made good. There existed between them the strongest affection and friendship. Victor had written letter after letter to his uncle begging to be permitted to enter college, or even to be placed in the counting-house, anything but the monotonous mildness, the feeble girlish existence under the charge of an aged clergyman, as if they were weak in the intellect. He never got a reply. Then he made various plans of escape; but the question always came, what could he do without money? So the time went on till Victor was twenty-two and Francis twenty-one. Then a violent fit of restlessness seized

Victor, and he persuaded Francis to join him despite of the other's scruples. If they could not permanently escape, they could at least have a month or two of 'lark' in France. Victor's plan was to wait till their next quarter's allowance came, and then bolt. This they did without the slightest trouble. They went to London, and from there started for Paris *viâ* Dover. In the train they fell in with half-a-dozen very agreeable fellows, who produced some champagne and a pack of cards. Now if there was one thing more severely forbidden at the tutor's than another it was every form of gambling. In consequence it had irresistible attractions—even the mild and good Francis could not help it. They played the whole journey, and arrived at Dover station with one pound ten out of forty pounds with which they started. The half-a-dozen agreeable gentlemen were in fact card-sharpers, and had an easy prey. Francis, in an agony of remorse, was for returning on foot with that small sum of thirty shillings, begging pardon, and being reinstated. Victor

would hear of no such thing—he had started
to see France, and see France he would. Half
by threat and half by ridicule he overcame
Francis's reluctance, and they went to a pawn-
broker's to pawn their watches. Just as they
entered the shop two men pounced on them
and held them fast. They were detectives in
plain clothes. A great jewel robbery had
been recently committed. Francis turned
pale, not so much with affright as with
shame. Victor laughed, and went willingly
to the superintendent of police. A few questions from him elicited the fact that they were
no thieves, and they were allowed their liberty.
Francis pleaded hard to return. Victor shook
him and called him a milksop. He boldly
marched back to the pawn-shop and got five
pounds on their watches, about one-sixth of
their value. Then they inquired about the
steamer—the last had been gone about two
hours ; there was no other boat that night.
Nothing daunted, Victor 'dragged Francis
down to the beach, and hired a sailing boat,
in which they actually crossed the Channel,

sick as dogs, and got into Calais about one in the morning. The cash left, after paying the boatman, was about two pounds. They slept at a cabaret, where the chambermaid and maid-of-all-work laughed in their faces when they complained of the extreme narrowness of the bed, and demanded four francs overnight. Next morning they started to walk to Paris. They got over four hours on one of those straight and endless military roads with the poplars on each side, and then, tired and weary and hungry, looked round in vain for refreshments. A peasant at his dinner saw them staring about, and immediately sprang up and rushed out to offer his assistance. They asked for dinner; he took them in; they found the soup admirable, and the good man grateful for the five-franc piece they gave him. Had it been an English labourer's cottage they would have starved on sour cheese and bread. Here they feasted on delicious soup, and set out strong and refreshed. But that was not all. Jacques assured them that they were not on the straight road to Paris—monsieur must cross the country to the right, and get into the Abbeville track; that would save twenty miles. He would show them. They followed his directions, and left the hard and beaten road. They walked on briskly for a couple of hours. The track had dwindled down now to a bridle-path; then it enlarged into a lane; presently it fell to a foot-path, and they were again tired and hungry. There was nothing in sight but ploughed fields and a few willow-trees. A hundred yards farther on and the foot-path ended in a sandy field with a few bushes of furze. Pushing on through this they entered a common minus a road or path at all. This was encouraging at four in the afternoon and the clouds threatening rain. It was late in the autumn, Michaelmas, and the sun was getting low. The prospect was anything but cheering. Poor Francis was in misery. His feet were blistered, and his conscience pricked him. This was the reward of wrong-doing. They should have to spend a night in the open air.

Exhausted, at last they sat down under a low wall. Victor was still strong and ready to march, but feebler Francis was completely done up. All they could do was to sit still and bewail their fate, which was night and damp shirts, as the black cloud yonder prophesied but too plainly.

While they were sitting here disconsolately they became conscious of a most singular and unaccountable noise. It was not the crowing of cocks and hens, nor the mewing of cats, nor the barking and yelping of puppies, and yet it seemed like the first attempt at language by the young of some animal. Neither of them could make it out. Francis had a weakness for pets, and he had kept most animals, and he was quite sure it was none of them. A most extraordinary and remarkable row—such a cackling, and crowing, and yelping, and shrill crying. Nothing like it ever assailed mortal ears before. They listened for some time, making all sorts of conjectures. Then Victor resolved to penetrate the obscurity, to ' thrust the mystery carte and tierce.' Francis begged him to remember that there were wolves in France even now; those might be the cries of the cubs. Victor laughed him to scorn, and sprang over the wall. He disappeared round a thicket, and came back in ten minutes shaking with laughter. 'What fools we have been!' he said; 'come and see.' Rather unwillingly Francis got over the wall and limped after him. Victor took him round the thicket, and pointed. It was a curious spectacle.

There was a large rambling house, tiled and rather dreary looking, though pierced with innumerable windows. In front of it, and reaching almost to their feet, was a broad lawn closely mown and well kept. On this lawn about one hundred babies, at the lowest calculation, were tumbling, walking, jumping, fighting, scratching, yelling, and generally amusing themselves with true infant glee. Two or three women were slowly walking up and down side paths, busily knitting as they went. This was the cause of the noise which had alarmed them. No wonder they could not make it out. They watched the scene for a few minutes. Presently a bell rang, and as if by magic all the troop began to toddle towards the house, in which one and all disappeared.

'Well,' said Victor, 'I'll go back now, Francis, if you want; if we go a thousand miles we shall never beat this.'

But Francis was too footsore to attempt further walking. What was to be done? There was no other house within sight; clearly they must apply here for lodging and refreshment. Finally they walked round to the front door and hammered at the knocker. A servant took them into a well-furnished parlour, where in a minute or two 'monsieur' made his appearance. It was evident on his face that he was very much astonished at their appearance at his mansion, and that he did not know what to make of them; but he was extremely polite, and soon perceiving that they were evidently young men of position, possibly of wealth, he began to smell out a way in which they might be profitable. So he begged them to accept a bed and to partake of supper, and generally to make themselves at home. They did not like the look of the fellow, but there was no other alternative, for by this time the rain was pouring down in torrents. 'At least,' said Victor, when they were alone upstairs, 'I've got a penknife, and they can't rob us of much, at all events.'

'Monsieur' brought out some wine after supper. Victor, always bold and inquiring, asked outright what was the meaning of all these children, despite Francis's frantic signs to him to hold his tongue and make as if they were quite ignorant. 'Monsieur' was delighted to give any information—he would be proud to show them over his establishment. He assured them upon his faith and his God that his beds were perfectly clean and wholesome, and his system humane in the extreme. *They* were well fed, well dressed, well cared for by good nurses; what more did they want? If anything, they had a good garden to play in; and when they grew bigger—

'But how the devil do they get here?' burst in Victor, interrupting the torrent of loquacity.

Ah, that was a good joke. Monsieur was really too good—and a young man too (meant to be a wicked joke). It was a form of maladie Anglaise.

'You don't mean to say these infants are English?'

Ma foi, but they were though, every single one of them.

'And how the deuce do they get here, and whom do they belong to?'

'Well, they arrived in the world in various vague ways.'

But a hint was enough; he need say no more. They were well cared for, and their papas and mammas could move in good society, and no one the wiser. Que voulez-vous? They had an agency in London. Monsieur could see it in the daily papers. Here was a copy.

Victor read: 'Private agency, No. — T— Road. Charges moderate. Strict confidence. No inquiries.'

Francis, sickened at this horrible recital of cold-blooded wickedness, nudged Victor to silence; but Victor would not till he had mastered the whole detestable system in its details.

Monsieur felt himself a benefactor to his species — it made him feel so large-hearted and benevolent to see these tiny creatures luxuriating in his abode. Perhaps another day his guests would recommend him; perhaps—

They slept there that night. In the morning they went back to Calais, and reached the tutor's with sixpence left. The establishment they had discovered was kept a profound secret between them.

Francis tried to forget all about it. Not so Victor. He pondered. He was a young man of ideas. He evolved a plan out of this discovery.

At this date he was free—he was twenty.

five — he had come into his share of the ninety-five thousand pounds under certain restrictions. Francis had another year to wait ; but they permitted him to live with his brother in chambers in Curzon-street.

Victor had already applied his idea. He had succeeded in persuading Maud into the belief that it was an accurate and practicable one.

Maud was Carlotta's lady housekeeper— this was her holiday time. She had risen to be a lady housekeeper after five-and-twenty years of governess life.

CHAPTER X.

Louis began to hate Heloise; not passively and
negatively, but actively. She was a tie upon
him; but it was not that altogether. It was
the consciousness that her whole life and
nature was a reflection upon *his*. Her purity
and truth and innocence were a slur upon him
and his ways. He hated her. The galling
knowledge that he could not escape from the
fetters binding him to her added to his passion. He considered how he could get rid of
her. There were but two methods, death or
divorce. He could murder her, but he
gnashed his teeth as he thought that it was
out of his power to divorce her. He could
kill her—he would not have hesitated at that.
A man who had associated with all the black-
guards in Europe, and with all the rowdies
of America, could not be supposed to possess
any terrors of conscience. He thought over

the idea thoroughly, and dismissed it as impracticable. There were so many obstacles in the way in this country of civilisation. He believed he could do it easily enough, and escape detection long enough to enable him to get abroad and hide. But that was not what he wanted. Such means as that would defeat the end in view. He wanted to remain in England. He had no idea of being hunted over the earth like a human hare—and he reflected that the world was so small nowadays. The electric telegraph had spanned the globe, and brought California and Australia within easy communication. The express train and the fast steamer had so narrowed the expanse between one country and another, that in point of fact the space of the world contracted day by day. It was so wretchedly small. There was no place a man could get to where he could not be got at in a very little time. But apart from that he did not wish to leave the society he usually moved in.

No. So far as he could see at present it

would not pay him to murder Heloise. This man calmly worked out this conclusion, as he smoked a cigarette, much as he would have worked out a monetary calculation as to the probable rise or fall of the funds. He was so utterly devoid of conscience that it never occurred to him to review the extreme wickedness of his reflections. There are those who may doubt that such a state of mind as this can possibly exist. They may say that the most hardened criminal feels remorse at times. It is possible that the most hardened criminal does, because such men are generally very ill educated and consequently superstitious. But Louis was highly educated, and superstition had no terrors for him. Moreover he had lived all his life in a groove corresponding to what his nature considered rational; in other words he had been 'faithful to the logic of his type' all his life. Therefore he felt no prick of conscience. He was, on the contrary, rather disgusted with the conclusion he came to. It would not pay to kill Heloise.

There only remained the alternative of divorce. So soon as he thought of that the remembrance of her truth and purity rose up and lashed him into a state of perfect fury. He had no grounds for a divorce. He could find no blame with her. She was so completely innocent, that even his evil mind could find no fault with her. There was not the slightest handle to lay hold of. But Louis, with all his temper, was a reflective man, and a philosopher after his kind. He reflected that if a handle did not exist, perhaps it was possible to make one. He reflected that even the purest and noblest minds are not always proof against temptation. He argued that in a certain 'set' there was no game considered so perfectly open and to afford such sport as a young married lady possessed of superior personal attractions. Suppose he threw her open to the efforts of these noble huntsmen? He growled as he remembered that Heloise was not made of the sort of stuff to fall a victim to their attentions. But fall a victim she should He, her husband, would ruin her, and then

out of that ruin, disgrace, and shame obtain
his freedom. This was a very pretty plan;
the only difficulty was to put it into practice.
Where was he to obtain the tempter? Where
could he find a man of sufficient attractions
or sufficient subtlety to reduce Heloise from
her normal path into one of misery and disgrace? He thought over every person of his
acquaintance, and was compelled to own that
there was none that he knew of. Still he
believed in the infinite possibilities of time.
Such a man would turn up if only he watched
and waited. Meantime he must endure the
bondage. This chafed and irritated him to
an unendurable degree. As it was entirely
his own fault, as he had himself for months
studiously endeavoured by all the means in his
power to induce Heloise to marry him, and as
he had therefore no one to blame but himself,
it followed as a matter of course that he must
find some one else to wreak his rage and ill-
temper on. Off he went to Carlotta.

That magnificent tigress received him
with a haughty toss of the head.

'It was your cursed fault,' he began; 'you persuaded me to marry her.'

She only sneered.

'You said it would allow us to be together more frequently, and with less suspicion. Who could find fault with the visits of a brother-in-law? She was to be our shield, under cover of which we—'

'We! You mean yourself.'

Louis stamped his foot with rage.

'Yes, *we!*' he reiterated. 'That *we* might enjoy an unfettered intercourse without fear of that fellow Horton—'

'In order that *you* might have the pleasure of contributing to my gratification, I certainly did favour your marriage with Heloise.'

'O, you did, did you? Really how kind, how considerate! Then *my* pleasure was of no account?'

'Certainly not; *you* never entered into my calculation. Poor fellow! did he quarrel with his toy? Should have another—he should, dear little boy!'

'You are an unnatural monster!'

'Am I really? How charming—a new sensation! You have forgotten falling in love with baby-face, I suppose? Who was it followed her about like a puppy at her heels? Who was it hung on her lips and drank her lisping words? Who rode with her? danced with her? sang with her? Who asked my assistance to secure her?'

Carlotta's eyes flashed, and her bosom heaved, as she hissed out her words.

'You double-dyed traitor! I help you! yes, I helped you! I persuaded Heloise, I urged Pierce into accepting you. I hushed up those ugly tales that floated about of your doings in order that you might marry my sister, that, as I foresaw, you might hate her and writhe under her yoke, and come to me and beg a little of my love. Psha! you mean-spirited fool, I spurn you!'

Louis looked wildly about him for a few minutes, as if he had been struck by apoplexy, and then rushed out. He found his way home mechanically. He met Heloise as he passed

through the dining-room, for it was close upon
six o'clock. Alarmed at his livid face, she
started and asked if he was ill.

'Go to the devil!' was his reply as he struck
her full in the face with his clenched hand; and
she fell senseless on the carpet. The sound of
her fall brought him to himself; he seized the
water on the table and dashed some in her
face, sneering as he observed the blood issuing
from her cut lip. He rang the bell, and told
the servants that their mistress had had a fit;
let them carry her up-stairs, and send for
Georgiana Knoyle, he added. 'Let her console
her,' he said to himself as he went up-stairs. 'A
new argument for her precious theories. What
a brute they will make me out! Stay!' An
idea struck him and he paused upon the stairs.
She might get a divorce from him as much as
he from her if he misbehaved himself—that
was a new idea—for cruelty, unfaithfulness,
desertion. Very good; he would give her
plenty of chances. This blow would make a
good beginning. He dressed carefully for
dinner, and had it all by himself in state, a

thing he rarely ever did. He heard that Georgiana had arrived. 'Now the folly will begin,' he said to himself. He called for his favourite wine, and sipped it with gusto. He would call on Carlotta again in the evening—not before nine. He would tell her of the little incident, it would amuse her. He drank more wine. The magnificent vixen, she was jealous, ha, ha! More wine. Jealous of his love for Heloise in that summer at Avonbourne. She was a splendid woman—a grand creature—free of all those girlish airs and prejudices. Jealous of him—that was consoling. She would never discard him. It revived his spirits. The extraordinary command the tiger had over her feelings—to actually encourage him to marry her sister, to do all in her power to accelerate the match, and then to calmly wait for the inevitable result—for the discord, and the cruelty, and unfaithfulness. He chuckled as he thought of it. There was no one like Carlotta. A grand creature. He admired her subtlety. A boa-constrictor in female form. What a pleasure there was in playing with the tigress! He would go and see her again in an hour or two.

Just then the footman entered, bringing in a telegram. Louis tore it open. It ran thus:

'*Horton Knoyle, Grand Hôtel, Paris, to Louis Fontenoy, No. — G——square, London.*

'Come over at once. Shebang has arrived.'

Louis sprang up, seized his hat, called a cab, and drove to the London, Chatham, and Dover. The tidal train for the night steamer was at the platform with steam up. He took his ticket, and was *en route* in five minutes.

In America, when a man by the force of his character takes a certain amount of lead among his neighbours, they call him 'General,' or leader, just as in the olden time the head of a marauding expedition was called *dux bellorum*—the duke or leader of battle.

'General' Shebang was sitting with Horton Knoyle, Esq., financier, in the private apartments of the latter at the Grand Hôtel. They were in deep and earnest conversation. Shebang was no vulgar Yankee. He was a polished and polite gentleman. The only sign of the American was his boots. Somehow no foreigner can ever wear thoroughly English boots, try how he will.

Louis's theory was that you should never depend upon your friends to have dinner, or supper, or refreshment, or comfort of any kind, waiting for you. This was what vulgar people did. They imagined that their friends were so eagerly awaiting their arrival, that they had killed and cooked the fatted calf, and got everything ready and pleasant. When these ignorant fools arrived—tired, weary, dusty— they found their friends cool, calm, easy, and in a state of unostentatious repose, without a room ready, or anything eatable or drinkable. The man of the world took care of himself *en route*. He refreshed his inner man. He washed and dressed at the last railway station or hotel. He had his boots cleaned, and the dust re- moved. Thus he came in at the end of his journey as fresh, as presentable in every way, as comfortable, as if he only lived half a mile off. So Louis came into the Grand Hôtel ready for instant conversation. It was seven o'clock in the morning, but he had telegraphed from Calais that he was coming, and Knoyle was waiting for him, and *waiting alone.*

'Shebang is asleep,' said Knoyle immediately they had shaken hands. 'At least I have ascertained he is in his room. He will not rise till ten—we have three hours at least. You had better depart before he rises, for *they are keen.*'

'Very keen,' replied Louis. 'Now what does he propose?'

'He wants a million,' said Horton slowly, as if reflecting on Shebang's proposals. 'He wants a million in cash, and half of it at once. To guarantee that million, he and ninety-nine other gentlemen will mortgage their estates in Carolina, Alabama, and Louisiana, each to the extent of five thousand pounds. That would cover five hundred thousand pounds. They will each guarantee one thousand pounds per annum, or one hundred thousand pounds, *i.e.* interest at the rate of twenty per cent. The other half-million I am to guarantee shall be forthcoming if they succeed in holding the line west of the Mississippi for three months; and if it is not forthcoming, then I forfeit my mortgages and interest. So that in point of fact I must hold the other five hundred thousand pounds ready in the bank, and so lose interest upon it. This reduces the interest they pay me to ten per cent. On final success the draft agreement (I will show it to you in a minute) provides that I take the sole monopoly of cotton exports for five years, and they repay me in full, which, according to their calculation, ought to give me a million over my outlay. Now the question is, can these men be trusted? We have conversed on this matter before. I have sent for you now to have your final opinion. Also I want your opinion on the condition of the public mind in the States. I know you are well acquainted with the inner life of the cities' (there was a slight accent of a sneer in the remark, but so slight as to be barely perceptible). 'These men, you see, have estates—enormous estates —but they have no ready money, the last war took it all—there's where they are beaten. The question is, if they had the ready money, and spent it judiciously, is their propaganda likely to meet with popular favour south and west?'

'Of this I am quite certain,' replied Louis: 'the South, as it rises from the effects of the war, and regains its old wealth and political coherence, has, and still further will, unite itself with the vigorous and thriving West. Hitherto all the traffic—the enormous goods and grain traffic—of the West has passed through the Northern States, and been shipped at Northern ports; it was carried on Northern lines, built by Northern enterprise. But the companies, exhilarated at the success of the North in the war, and confident of a monopoly, have so risen their charges for transit, that the cost of carriage clogs the enterprise of the Western people. Consequently there exists the bitterest animosity against them and against the Legislature, which, Northern in its sympathies, will afford no redress. Hence the West gravitates hourly towards the South, and the South, rising again, seeks an ally in the West. The movement is national in its magnitude, but hitherto it has been under the surface. If a leader or band of leaders sprang up, without doubt both South and West would rise; and the train could easily be fired down South by exciting the race-hatred of whites to blacks.'

'Shebang,' said Horton, 'thinks that Cuba would join the South, with the idea of curbing the North, and retaining slavery. There is a grandeur about the scheme of uniting the South and West in a great autonomic republic exceedingly captivating to my mind. And Europe is so overdone, there is no market for money. The old monarchs have borrowed and borrowed, till they are waist-deep in debt; their loans are merely makeshifts to pay the coupons on old debts. I want something new, fresh, with a prospect of vigorous extension. Much depends upon the personal character of these gentlemen. You are acquainted with Shebang and the rest or most of them.'

Louis entered into a rapid but graphic

picture of the character and lives of these men. He painted them as they were, and he did not spare their evil traits. On the whole it was satisfactory.

'But still,' continued Horton, 'there remains to be considered the *hands* for the work. What of the men they propose to employ—the agents, the military adventurers? Of what stuff are these made?'

Louis described them as desperate in the extreme. Horton asked if there was not a suspicion of Communism amongst them. Louis admitted that there was.

'I like a little Communism,' said Horton thoughtfully. 'That affair in this Paris did me a great deal of good. The monarchs had got into a way of thinking themselves quite safe; they were growing insolent, they even attempted to drive terms with us capitalists. Fancy that! *Now* they feel their lack of stability—they are courteous, they pay us attention, they take *our* terms. Ah, I am not sure that the establishment of another republic would not make them still more anxious to retain our good-will. I will not detain you longer—Shebang will be down in ten minutes. Adieu ; remember me to Heloise.'

There was a smile on the lips of both the men as they parted. There was a very different expression when the door closed between them. ' He *must* suspect, he *must* know something at least,' reflected Louis, as he walked out into the city of Napoleon. ' So deep and penetrating a mind cannot but suspect, even if nothing more; but I am useful to him—he will make no noise, no disturbance, while I play into his hands; while I increase his wealth with my knowledge I am safe with Carlotta.'

Horton was pondering too. His question was—would Louis deceive him ? Had he a motive, an interest to do so ? Considering the peculiar relations which existed (a spasm of pain passed over his forehead), he hardly thought so. No; Louis could be trusted not to quarrel with his own interest.

Thus they plotted and schemed and wove their webs, while poor Heloise lay at home in a darkened room, frenzied with fever, tended by patient loving Georgie. The doctors said her lip — her mobile, beautiful lip — would show a scar to her dying day, even if she rose from the bed of fever. They industriously spread the report that it was a fall in a fit. Georgie reflected upon this 'little incident,' as Louis called it, as she sat by the bedside. Was marriage so divine an institution? Could she trust herself even with Neville irrevocably and for ever? It was a deep and an anxious question to her. It almost seemed as if the irresponsible power given to a man by marriage acted as the heat of a conservatory to force up and strengthen the growth of the evil passions of his nature. The sense of irresponsibility seemed to remove all the restraints of society, and all the dormant evil burst out. There appeared to be almost a curse upon it. And poor Horton too, and *that* Carlotta! It was a most sad and serious thing. Could nothing be done to alter this—to evade this terrible fatality attending marriage? How was it possible to amend that institution?

CHAPTER XI.

Louis, by an impulse, when he left Horton did not return at once to England. He took the train almost immediately for Brussels. The air of the Continent, the indefinable influence of the well-remembered architecture, the very sound of the language, acting through old associations, brought up an irresistible desire to visit and confer with his old companions. He slept almost the whole of the journey. He could have gone on at once from Brussels to Antwerp, but he preferred to stay an hour or so for refreshment. Then he started again. It was night when he began to pick his way on foot through the jungle of streets and corners, the convoluted congeries of houses which constitutes the city of Rubens. He had not come to study the works of that great artist. But even in Rubens' day

Antwerp produced that fleshly sensuous style of beauty which is one of its chief, though unacknowledged, attractions in this modern time. Louis strolled leisurely along, and entered a large glass door flaringly illuminated. On the right, as he entered, he saw through the panes of another glass door an enormous room surrounded with sofas of red velvet, upon which a numerous company of handsome and well-dressed ladies were sitting, attended by knots of gentlemen. He passed these attractions, and ascended the staircase, threading a maze of galleries with evident familiarity, till at the end of a narrow corridor lighted by a stained-glass window he was stopped by a gentleman, who extended his arm across the passage. Louis smiled, bowed, and whispered a single word. The arm was withdrawn, a door flung open, and he entered a small apartment, where five or six persons were seated round a table upon which was wine and fruit. It was only a conversation, it was not a consultation night, to Louis's regret. Nevertheless he sat down, neither of the party taking the slightest notice of him. He helped himself to wine, none of the rest even so much as pausing a moment in their remarks.

'I do not agree with you,' said Grousset, a Frenchman; 'I think London most easily assailable. A city that is mined underneath from one end to the other must always be an easy prey. All that you require is to fire the gas-pipes in twenty different places, and blow it up.'

'Or,' continued Pasqui, an Italian, 'you can obtain access to the sewers, which are enormous in London, and fill them with nitro-glycerine; about five tons' weight of that substance would throw the city into the air.'

'Mere nothings to what I would suggest,' interrupted a Prussian. 'I would dam up the sewers, and shut off the escape of the solid and liquid sewage into the river. When a certain district, where the occupation of the inhabitants was principally keeping horses for hire— mews I think they call it—was declared infected with some disease, it was ordered that no manure or other refuse should be carted out of it. The heaps accumulated, and in ten days the whole place was attacked with diarrhœa, which decimated the inhabitants. A hostile fleet has, therefore, simply to dam up the sewers and prevent the outflow of noxious matter ; the accumulation of this matter, and the penetration of poisonous gases into the houses, would, in a fortnight, infect the whole metropolis with typhus fever and cholera.'

'A sublime idea, by which slops would conquer heroes,' cried Grousset.

'I would take England with three hundred resolute men,' said Prognowski, a Russian; 'such men, I mean, as Peter the Great commanded, who would throw themselves off a tower into eternity for his pleasure. All you want is three hundred such fellows, and a swift steamer. I see an English firm offers to build a steamer which shall travel twenty-five miles an hour. Where is the cumbrous ram or the swift clipper that could overtake such a vessel as that? Let fifty of the men land on the Isle of Wight, where the English Queen walks about unattended, and seizing her and one or two of the family, carry them off to the steamer. At the same moment, the two hundred and fifty men, conveyed by train to London, and utterly unnoticed in the vast multitudes who exist there, seize the Bank of England, where thirty million pounds in hard gold are deposited. It would be essential to hang some court official at the yard-arm of the steamer, to enforce the threat of destroying the Royal Family if the two hundred and fifty men in possession of the Bank were not allowed to depart in peaceful procession, carrying with them the stores of bullion in the cellars. The English troops would protect them from the fury of the populace, lest the royal party should suffer. Once on board the steamer with their bullion and away, who could catch them?'

' And where could they go?' asked Louis with a sneer. ' What country could they fly to where the telegraph would not anticipate their arrival?'

' O,' replied Prognowski, ' I spoke supposing some nation was at war with Great Britain. By removing the thirty million pounds in the Bank cellars the backbone of England would be broken; for although her patriot soldiers might possibly fight without pay, it would be impossible to transport them, to concentrate them, or to provide them with provisions without money.'

'The object of destroying England I cannot see,' said an American. 'It is from England that we derive the money which is essential to our projects. If she collapsed, where should we get the necessary funds? Depend upon it, no continental nation will engage in war with Great Britain. They may foam at the mouth, and curse the English, but they know full well that their interest demands that England should be prosperous. What would their governments do without the English capitalist? Who paid the expenses of the French war, thereby liberating French territory and indemnifying the Germans? It was the English capitalist. Who supports the tottering cabinet of Vienna, the conspiracy-frightened cabinet at St. Petersburg, who props up France, and even keeps Spain from total ruin? The English capitalist. As for Italy, her existence depends upon the London Stock Exchange. England is necessary to the world.'

'Talking of continental politics,' said Grousset, 'I am certain that Bismarck corresponds with the Prince Imperial. The astute old German looks upon the restoration of the Napoleons as a mere question of time. The Prince Imperial and his advisers would be delighted to see Bismarck tighten his reins, and give a check, that he might pose himself as a leader, as the representative of popular indignation. Bismarck wants the Republic destroyed.'

'He must take care, or he will find a republic in Germany spring up under his very feet,' said the Prussian. 'It is just possible that while the war-fever lasts, and men see that leaders are necessary, that they will endure the iron rule of the Government. But let once there be a prospect of peace, and down go king and kaiser, and up goes a republic. There is no animosity between the great republican leaders on either side of the Rhine. I know as a fact that the republicans in France are at this moment considering on the draft of an agreement between them and the republicans of the states of the German Empire. That agreement stipulates that in consideration of the return of Alsace and Lorraine, the French shall support the uprising of the German people in favour of a republic.'

'Our society,' said the American, 'requires neither monarchy nor republic. The one is as fatal to our designs and belief as the other. Our one grand fundamental doctrine is the supremacy of natural genius.' ('Hear, hear!' and applause.) 'Now the existence of a monarchy totally deprives genius of its natural supremacy, since the head of the state is hereditary, and the greatest talent cannot elevate the possessor to that position. Now the republic supposes a president who is as frequently elected by the jarring factions of ignorance as from any true ability he possesses ; and when once he fills that place, there is no room for another. What we truly want, then, is neither a monarchy nor a republic ; nor is it precisely the commune. The commune, it is true—-the local self-government of innumerable small districts—gives an opportunity to the genius of each district to assert itself, and take its natural preëminence. That is so far good, and what we wish. But there is something further than this. Theoretically, the perfect man needs no government at all. He is his own king, his own lawyer, his own priest, almost his own Deity. He requires no king to command or compel him to obey the laws, because he follows them from his own appreciation of their application to the good of society; no lawyer to expound these laws, or apply them, because he thoroughly understands the spirit of them ; and in such a state equity, and not precedent, supplies the rule of judgment. No priest, because he sees clearly the relation between God and man ; no Deity, because even if God did not exist, so strong is his belief in the beauty of the social relations, and in the sublime mission of man, he would still remain truthful, upright, grand, and noble, and worthy of immortality, even if there were no such thing as a hereafter. When, through education and the progress of time, every man in this great and populous globe shall arrive at such an elevated state of mind as this, it is evident that no government could be required. Thus, therefore, neither monarchy nor republic nor commune would be required ; but still there must remain a certain degree of difference between men.

'Men would still be born who possessed a greater share of talent and genius than their friends and the surrounding population. These, without any sign or badge of distinction, or any power of executing their ideas, must still occupy the position of mental leaders of the population, much as in the early days of the Hebrew constitution the prophets, without any legal status, exercised a great influence upon the affairs of that remarkable nation. This, I think, is our doctrine in outline.' (Applause.)

'For many years,' said an old man, who had hitherto been silent, 'I have revolved in my mind the idea of founding an intellectual priesthood, after the model of the priesthood of Rome, with various degrees of deacon, priest, cure, archdeacon, bishop, archbishop, cardinal, and lastly, a head answering to the Roman pope ; which intellectual priesthood should at once educate the masses, govern them, and afford to the talent and genius of the earth a true and certain method of rising to their natural level : the greatest intellect, the greatest genius taking the position of head or pope.'

'I differ from you entirely,' said Grousset, 'and for simple reasons. The machinery in time would forget the great cause for which it was instituted, and would live for and study Itself only, just as the Roman priesthood, originally instituted for the best of ends, finally came to be what we see it now—an order seeking only its own elevation, at the expense of truth and of liberty.'

'No, I think it much better that we should

remain as we are now,' said the American, 'without organisation properly so called, scattered all over the world. In that very want of organisation our power, which is derived from our originality, exists. And so soon as one of our order succeeds in realising his idea—let it be mechanical, let it be mental or moral, let it be what it may—we one and all, in various quarters of the globe, rush forward to assist and aid him. In the rude and rough press of Western America appear articles praising and glorifying our friend and his attempt; in the civilised cities of Europe books and pamphlets, lectures and meetings, demonstrate the worth of the new prophet who has arisen. We propagate the idea everywhere. We are bound together by an electric sympathy only, but that sympathy is the strongest bond of all.'

'Well,' said Louis, rising to speak, 'I have news for you all. One of our order has succeeded in realising his idea; it will be your duty to hasten to assist him. At this very hour General Shebang and the millionnaire at

Paris are exchanging the ratifications of the treaty which secures Shebang a million sterling to unite the South and West in one grand republic !'

A cheer greeted this announcement.

'They ridiculed Napoleon,' said Grousset, 'because he went to war for an idea. The fools ! All the nations of the earth had previously gone to war. For what? Out of hatred and envy and jealousy—out of prejudice—for varying creeds and religious difference—to revenge imaginary insults, or to add to their own glory and power.

'But Napoleon had neither hatred, envy, or jealousy, or creed, as his animating motive. None of the base passions and the feeble prejudices of the world influenced him. He warred for an idea. It was a grand spectacle; it was the act of a Genius. It was no wish of his to spill blood, or to kill a single man. But he had an idea; he had a conception. To carry that idea into execution it was necessary to make war, and he made it. It was the only justifiable war that ever was made. But it illustrates another side of our doctrine and order. We do not hesitate at blood, or at murder, or at force, or any other act which prejudice calls crime, in order to carry out our idea. Thus Samuel hewed Agag in pieces in cold blood in order to secure the execution of his idea, which was an Israel free from idolatry. Thus, if one of our order divulges our secrets, he is removed by knife or by surer means. To us there is no crime. Crime does not exist to us ; we are above it. It is impossible that our hands should commit it. Our ideas render our actions sacred.'

A slight smile passed over Louis's countenance. His eyes were fixed upon the speaker, studying him with delicious relish. This last sentiment was *caviare* to him. It was exquisite to see men who professed the highest aims, and the deification of the human race, declare that if they imbrued their hands in blood it was no more than as if they had washed them in water. It was a union of the divine with the diabolical which exactly suited his appetite. He left them to their wine and to their conversation and repaired to his hotel, not without a certain uneasiness in his own mind. There was some danger in belonging to this order. He knew full well that they possessed means of carrying out their threats little dreamt of by those in authority. He knew that no man's life, upon whom their enmity was fixed, was safe for an instant. It was true that at present he was upon excellent terms with them. But he was conscious that in the secret recesses of his own mind a half-formed design had been lingering of late to use them to his own purpose, a use which they might call betrayal. Still he laughed the momentary oppression off, and turned his thoughts upon Carlotta, whom he should see upon the morrow. He sailed next morning straight for London in the steamer.

CHAPTER XII.

THERE are many of our friends who will gather round us in the first flush of an accident, or of an illness, or of the incidence of misfortune; there are few—very few—who remain after their curiosity is satisfied, and they can say, 'Well, we have done what we could.' Even the devoted friend who has nursed us through a desperate illness will leave us as we are getting better, leave us to the long restless hours of convalescence. But Georgie, true sterling Georgie, remained with Heloise not only through fever and prostration, but through the weary endless hours the invalid could only lie on her sofa next the window, and watch the shifting clouds. As she was almost always with Heloise it followed that Neville Brandon, her lover, came here to see her. What was more natural?

But Neville had a brother, and he too came and was introduced to Heloise. That brother was the very Noel Louis had taunted Carlotta about, and showed his angry jealousy. Thus it is that one cause or one circumstance leads up to another, and effect follows cause, and cause again follows effect, though no one at the time ever dreamt of the ultimate result of the very natural and simple chain of commonplace circumstances.

This Noel Brandon was the battered warrior whom Carlotta had favoured with her smile, and thereby excited Louis's rage. He was not very battered either; but jealousy can see spots upon the sun. A small piece had been shot out of one ear, but the deficiency, not large in itself, was hidden by the curling brown hair. There was a broad scar on his neck, where a spear had penetrated and cut a deep gash, but it was hidden, or nearly so, by the shirt-collar. His left arm was sometimes in a sling, especially in cold damp weather ; it was the effect of an old musket-shot. His nose was not slit ; that was purely an addition of Louis's. He was dark by nature, and tanned, by the sun and by incessant exposure, to the hue of the darkest gipsy. But his brilliant black eye betrayed an intensity of animal life and vigour. His broad and massive shoulders, his brown and rather large hand, fitter for the sabre than the pen, the general air of strength and resolution which hovered over the man, spoke the inborn warrior, the Nimrod, the mighty hunter, not only of the timid deer, but of men. Yet he held no commission; he was no parchment captain, no spur-jingling colonel. His commission was issued by the inbred necessity which existed for him to fight. Fight he must, and fight he had from earliest childhood.

What a contrast there was between him and Neville! Never were two brothers so utterly unlike. Neville was all thought, contemplation; Noel was all deed. They had both been great travellers; one at least had been a great explorer. But Neville had always halted on the verge. He sought the primeval forests of America, that he might

commune with Nature in her oldest aspect.
But he penetrated a few miles only. Then
he sat down and thought. The narrow belt
of trees between him and the nearest cultivated plot was as deep a seclusion to him as
if it had been a thousand miles in breadth.
He retired within himself; he forgot all things
but Nature, and Nature entered in, and per-
meated him. But Noel sprang forward, rifle in
hand, and, firing at beasts and Indians alike,
pushed his way across to the Rocky Mountains. Seized with an uncontrollable desire to
investigate the origin of the mysterious Nile,
Neville departed for Egypt. But he paused
at the cataracts, on the very edge of the
desert. Then again he sat down—and thought.
The influence of the ocean of sand, the illimitable expanse of innumerable atoms, entered in
and dwelt in his mind. His mental eye saw
over and under and round about it, and saw
things which the physical eye suspected not.
But Noel went out straight into the desert
almost alone—straight as an arrow, southwards, ever southwards, right down through

the centre of Africa, till he reached the Cape of Good Hope. A stupendous journey, of which he thought and said and wrote nothing, not a word. He replied to one questioner, that the one thing he did was to 'Push on.' That was his secret. He had no other. Those who wished to know what was in the interior of equatorial Africa could go and follow his track and see for themselves. He should write not a line; look at his hand, how could he? the fingers were stiff from the use of the rifle. The way was open to all—let them go. The secret was 'Push on.'

Neville threw himself down to rest upon the beach, and listened to the surge, and thought. Noel swam out, with his bold breast fronting the waves—out, and still out, till his head was hardly visible. Yet it is a question which had seen the most. Noel had been over the most ground. But Neville had apparently seen as much in a limited space. The secrets of the interior of the forest, the desert, and the ocean, seemed of their own accord to seek him as he sat upon the edge.

Calmly and with divine repose he collected them, and stored them up in the treasure of his mind; ever seeking to discover the true relation of man to nature, ever seeking to discover the attributes of the Great Soul which had called the world into existence.

Almost the one regret of Noel's life was that he had been away, and had not been with the Italian army when finally they entered Rome. He would have given the whole fortune he possessed—no small one—to have marched into the Eternal City one of the soldiers of truth and liberty. It was the one regret of his life.

Almost the one regret of Neville's life was that he never had time enough. People said he was leisurely, even lazy, indolent; that he lingered over things that others passed by in a few minutes. But his complaint was that he never had time enough. He was always hurried away by circumstances just as he was beginning to see—just as his eyes got accustomed to the darkness, and he could penetrate into the unknown. It was so with life. He mourned its shortness. He should never have time enough.

Thus the soldier who fought for truth regretted his absence from the active scene at a critical moment. Thus the scholar who thought and searched for truth regretted that Time was not long enough to study the works of his God, much less that God Himself.

There was a singular charm about both these men. They were so deeply, so intensely in earnest. There was no show, no stamping of the foot, no waving of the hands, no loud and angry controversy. But there was a depth, a latent resolution which insensibly impressed those who approached them.

Carlotta tried her best to induce Noel to publish his enormous journey through Africa; she knew that it would create a sensation; he must dedicate it to her; there would be an *éclat*. In vain; he paid no attention. This man saw Heloise. He saw too the mark of the cut upon her lip. Some fragment of the truth, despite all the care with which it was hidden, oozed out. Could he help but feel indignation? How could his heart, brave and generous as it was, help warming to this poor girl? Then Carlotta, hearing of it, also laughed at it, jeered at it, to him ; exulted in it. All the tiger jealousy in her burst out with fierce exultation. She triumphed in it. She gloated over it. Up till then Noel had been fascinated to some extent by her magnificent beauty; now he was disgusted. His eyes were opened ; he saw the venom beneath the many-coloured skin of the snake. He recoiled. His thoughts dwelt in consequence more upon Heloise.

Poor Heloise; those were very weary days to her. All her young life used to the free fresh air and ceaseless exercise, all her days spent in restless motion, now tied down to her chair with sheer weakness. Nothing more; the fever had left her, the scar upon the lip was healed, though the mark was ineffaceble. The physicians said that all she needed was strengthening food, and as soon as possible change. But it was slow, very slow. Sometimes the very weariness of waiting brought the unbidden tears to her eyes, and she leant her head back on Georgie's loving shoulder and wept silently. When first she rose, the leaves were brown and gold and scarlet upon the trees; now they were gone and the boughs were bare. The swallows had fled; she thought of Avonbourne; how dreary it would look now! Yet she loved it whenever so dreary. How she longed to see Pierce, 'dear papa!' He had been kept in utter ignorance of all this. 'Do not agitate his old age,' pleaded Heloise ; Georgie herself saw no good in it. Pierce therefore knew nothing of it, else he would have been instantly at her side.

And Louis? She did not hate him. She did not resent the cruel and unprovoked blow ; she did not recoil from the utter brutality of the man. She simply forgot him; with the blow that laid her senseless upon the carpet all memory of him fled. Not that she did not recollect his existence as a person; but he was no more Louis. He wiped himself out of the tablet of her mind at one stroke. He entered no more into her thoughts. It was as if he had never spoken to her, never come within ken of her vision. She never saw him now, he never approached her. Perhaps it was merciful that this strange forgetfulness of the injury she had sustained had come over her. It prevented her from dwelling upon it. It enabled her to turn her mind to other things, even to find amusement. But Louis was her husband no longer. He was a shadow of the Past which had fled and left no mark. She heard his name, but it brought up no vision in her mind.

There was at times a certain amount of pleasure in this convalescence, especially when she got a little stronger. There were pleasant reunions in the evenings. Heloise sat in the midst in her great arm-chair, well propped up and supported by cushions, as a queen in the centre of her court. Around her gathered Georgie and Neville, and sometimes, more frequently of late, the soldier Noel. Each, one and all, followed their own occupations —that was the convention. Georgie worked at her book, making extracts, writing.

Neville also worked—studying great tomes which he brought with him, the works of Cuvier and of Owen. Noel read a novel. Heloise cared not to read—she worked a little embroidery. They talked when they liked, each when an idea occurred to him or her, and all stayed to listen. But there was no effort to prolong a conversation. Only one common object animated them all by tacit consent—to amuse Heloise. Whoever hit upon a subject, or a discovery, or anything that could interest her, the work was stayed, the book placed on the table, and they joined to please her, to bring the smile to the pale cheek, and the sparkle into her large deep eyes.

And Noel—the restless soldier, the never-tired traveller, the wanderer through desert and forest—what of him? He sat still as a piece of furniture, fearful to move lest he should disturb her. His novel was a mere pretence. He cared for no novels. His eyes were for ever upon her; not always her face, but her dress, her foot, her hand, her work, the chair she sat in. But always Heloise.

The physicians said she was strong enough now to move. But still they delayed; for the early winter was coming on, and they feared the cold weather, the exposure, the possible damp. What they dreaded was consumption. At present she was free from the slightest taint. But a cold, a chill—no one could foresee its effect in her delicate state. So she was compelled to sigh in vain for Avonbourne.

Perhaps it was better,' she said; 'Pierce will not see me till I am strong; then he will not inquire too curiously.'

Why was it that Noel's wandering eye fixed itself so often upon the slender hand? why did he gaze so earnestly at that tiny toy which ornamented the third finger ? It was the wedding-ring—the small band of gold, of ductile gold, which he could crush like an egg flat in his strong fingers. But a band of iron, and adamant; a circle strong as the magic circle of the necromancer, which none could overleap. The strong man to whom the simoom of the desert, the spear of the Arab, the roar of the lion, was as nothing, quailed, recoiled, drew back before this piece of talismanic gold.

Never before had he paused; never, like Neville, halted on the edge. Now he stood at a distance abashed, afraid. For the first time in his life he questioned himself—for the first time doubted himself. Hitherto he had rushed headlong forward, without staying to calculate the cost or the consequences. Now the very same influence which beckoned him on also warned him away.

Those evenings were very happy to Heloise. They soothed her. She never stayed to think or analyse; her life glided on smoothly, and she gave no heed whither it tended. She had no thought beyond herself and her dear Georgie. At that time she lived, as it were, with Georgie and herself. There was no outward influence that she was conscious of; only she began to prattle and talk, as women will to each other, of Georgie's approaching marriage with Neville. It was time now to see about the *trousseau*, to begin to arrange the innumerable details of dress. Into this He-

loise was eager to enter. She did not notice
that Georgie seemed to avoid the subject.
All recollection of her own unfortunate example appeared to have died away from her
mind. She was eager to see Georgie united
with her lover and happy. She talked of it
incessantly when they were alone. Georgie
did not repulse this conversation, but she did
not encourage it. She listened thoughtfully,
she replied correctly ; but she never began,
she never continued, the remarks which Heloise had made. But at such times involuntarily Georgie's gaze fixed itself almost unconsciously upon the mark on her friend's lip—
the lately-healed scar, small, slight, but distinctly perceptible. Heloise little thought
that hardly a night passed over when Georgie's
eyes were not wet with passionate tears, when
she did not pray earnestly to Heaven for
guidance in this hour of perplexity. Her
very heart and soul clung to Neville with a
strength that nothing could shake. But marriage—marriage with Louis before her eyes
daily—was it strange that she shrank from

it ? And it was not altogether self. She really and truly believed in her own mission —a woman sent to women. As such was it her duty to set forth another example of yielding up her entire being to the uncontrolled and irresponsible rule of man ? Was it not rather her duty to defend her weak and feeble sex against this assumption of irresponsible power and its apparently inevitable effect ? If she herself yielded, how could she persuade others to stand out ? Of what avail was precept without practice ?

But there sat Neville before her eyes, handsome exceedingly, fair and comely, his heart her very own. It was a terrible struggle. Thus, on the one side, the Woman strove to suppress her natural feelings towards the man ; and upon the other, the Man (Noel) struggled with his rising feelings towards Heloise.

And Heloise was unconscious of both these inward battles.

CHAPTER XIII.

In the midst of her toilette Carlotta, wearied with the work of binding up her heavy hair, had fallen languidly upon the ottoman, flinging her nude arm negligently over a chair. In this semi-unconscious state of indolent repose, the peculiar power of her beauty was stronger even than when full dressed and in all the flow of her spirits and her stinging epigrammatic wit; for she had that species of wit which, though weak in itself, takes most — the wit *de société*, in the sense of *vers de société* — the light sparkling foam that bubbles on the champagne of conversation.

How is it there has never been written a 'vision of evil women,' as there was one of 'fair women'? For what has been the influence and what the charm of the good and noble compared with that of the subtly evil?

It was well said that the wicked had fairly earned their supremacy over the good in this world by their superior energy.

The devil is always at work. 'The night cometh when no man can work,' was not said of him. The parson and curate, the archdeacon and the bishop and the archbishop—all the army of the cathedral—sleep the sleep of the just, and dream dreams of a safe and peaceful flock. But the devil never goes to bed. He earns his power as lord of this world by dint of sheer hard work. He has had many historians. There was a catalogue of books written about him published the other day, itself quite a book. But wicked woman, the prime mover, the very soul of the world, has never had her history written yet. What a roll of distinguished names, stretching from when time itself began down to our own day! And over them all there hovers a singular glory—a magnetic influence—a phosphoric glow; and the memory of them lingers in the mind of man. Whence comes it, this irresistible attraction? for it is not all their beauty alone, great as that may be. Noble and faithful women have been beautiful too, even perhaps far more lovely; but never have they attained to the same effect.

Yes; she was very beautiful, this Carlotta. There was a sense of intense animal vigour, a latent *pantherism* about her. The full voluptuous contour of the form, the superb neck and bust, the head set almost defiantly in its balance, conveyed the impression of physical nature in its perfection and completeness. There was an animal grandeur about her. As she reposed now, with her eyes gazing steadily into vacancy, there arose in them a glittering phosphoric light, such as may be seen in the panther's prowling in the dusk. She was fascinating; but seen thus in the abandon of solitude, there was an indefinable *horror*, as it were, hovering over her, much as there is over the curling folds of a still serpent glowing in colours. It seemed as if her very slumber—her very repose—was an attitude chosen expressly to enable her to spring upon her victim, and fix her claws in him to the death. It was an unearthly beauty seen thus, without the consciousness of being observed.

One arm was thrown negligently over a chair. It was round and full and firm, white and smooth as the skin of the famous empress who bathed in the milk of five hundred she-asses to preserve the polish of her limbs. What is there so graceful, so love-inspiring as the arm of a handsome woman? This was an arm which, without bracelet, or any contrivance to give the proper apparent curve, might have rivalled the statues of antiquity. The flesh looked as firm as the very marble in which they are carved, yet to the touch it was softer than velvet, and sank into a dimple at the slightest pressure. There was a smoothness, a polish upon the surface of the skin as if rubbed with oil; and here and there the blue veins wandered around it. An arm such as would have taken a theatre by storm; how many of the shouting, cheering amphitheatre would have risked their necks to feel its warm endearing embrace!

There was no effort about Carlotta; no airs, no display; she needed none to attract attention. In the most crowded assemblies she was invariably in a *pose* of perfect complacency, calm; there was no striving after effect. Alone, and unseen, there was the same easy unconscious grace, the ineffable charm of which is greater than that of the most regular features.

Yet she was no longer young. But the very years which would have detracted from the shape of the many had but added to the perfection and completeness of this evil woman. There was a finish, a fulness about her to which youth aspired in vain. It was this very finish, this fulness which made almost a slave of Louis; a slave whom all the loveliness, the freshness, and the purity of Heloise could never retain. Her very age, her very worldliness, her astute cleverness, attracted him irresistibly. There was a sense of personal vanity gratified in walking with this woman—her chosen companion—in the path of flowery wickedness. He knew her thoroughly—he knew her venomous hatreds, her insatiable conceit, her unscrupulous mind —and he gloried in it. Gloried in the fact that she had stooped to him; that with all her cleverness, and worldliness, and insatiable vanity she had linked her arm with his. She too understood him well. She did not hide from herself his almost devilish delight in the evil side of human nature. She knew that he was no lover in the old and true sense. She knew him thoroughly, and she too gloried in the power of attaching him to herself. What was it, what glory was it, to attract the young and inexperienced, the foolish, and the still more foolish aged? But Louis was a Man: unutterably a bad and abandoned being, but no half-hearted chicken, no poor creature confined in narrow limits by creed or fear. There was a sense of power gratified in attracting him. A strange bond between them, it may be; but no less a real and effectual one. They did not spare each other. He cursed her freely, with all the foul-mouthed vulgarity and brutality he had imbibed in

the low saloons of cities. She quailed not,
nor even averted her glance. She stung him
to the quick with her bitter words and sneering insinuations. He had struck her before
now. That splendid arm lying negligently
over the arm of the chair had been bruised by
his blows, and shown the blue mark for many
a day. Then she would sit before the glass
and look at it and gloat over it. Such was
her power over him, that in his rage and jealousy she could make him forget his manhood,
forget that she was a woman. Perhaps it was
this occasional habit of striking Carlotta that
led him to hurl Heloise to the ground. And
she, Carlotta, had dug her nails into his flesh
till the blood spurted up, and relaxed not her
hold till Louis beat her off. He could have
shown the dint of her teeth and the print of her
sharp and pointed nails. At such moments how
intense and venomous was the hatred between
them! Yet two hours afterwards they were
more closely bound together than ever. Who
could fathom the conditions, the emotions of
rage and jealousy and hatred which crowded

through her mind when she found that Louis was in love with Heloise at Avonbourne, in those months when Horton went trout-fishing? She never said a word to him; she encouraged him; she aided him with all her subtle touches and insinuating persuasions. She entered into the warmest friendship with Heloise. She painted Louis in the highest colours. And all the while a red-hot jealousy, a maddening hatred, was consuming her. With that in her heart she gave Heloise the most splendid presents, and arranged her marriage breakfast, almost with her own hands and with a smile upon her countenance. She knew the inevitable result; she foresaw it as clearly as Cæsar Borgia could foresee the results of his plans. She knew that Heloise's very innocence, now so charming, would in a few months first pall upon and then disgust her fickle husband, stable only in his vices. She knew that Louis would as inevitably return to his allegiance to her. And thus with double bitterness and double gall she should pour the ashes and embers of misery over her sister, while at the same moment Louis would writhe under his yoke. And this had come to pass exactly as she had planned, and almost as precisely as if events had happened by her order. She had triumphed and glowed with exultation. She had gone about with her heart elate and her step elastic, swelling with self-satisfaction, as she trampled upon Heloise. The period of her glory culminated when Louis struck his wife to the earth, and marked her with an indelible scar. But even in that very hour the tide was slowly turning. From that incident dated the introduction of Noel to Heloise. Noel had been Carlotta's latest success. She had tied him to her heels—this storm-beaten and resolute man, whose fame was so great and so well earned. With a secret delight and a mischievous joy she was busied in making a fool of him; holding him up to the finger of society as her chattel and her toy. Hercules had all but abandoned his club. In a few more weeks his head would be slumbering in her lap. At this moment he saw Heloise.

From that date he came no more. Suddenly and without warning he left her and returned not again; not even for farewell. She did not reflect that her own indecent exhibition of pleasure in the domestic trouble of her own sister had disgusted him. Her familiarity with Louis had blunted her finer perceptions. She cast the blame wholly and solely upon Heloise. The embers of jealousy and hatred blew up again into a fierce and burning flame. Not that she cared so much about Noel himself. It was Heloise. Her patience, her purity, her innocence, were reproaches to her. They were foils showing off in contrast the darkness of her own character. She had fully expected that Heloise would have left Louis, would have returned to Avonbourne, perhaps would have even entered a suit for separation. But no; she gave no sign. She remained at Louis's house, silent, patient. This irritated and annoyed Carlotta. It seemed as if her darts, tipped with fire and stained with poison, fell broken and unheeded against this mere child. She chafed and raged inwardly. She had never intended that Heloise and her affairs should become so prominent a subject in her daily thoughts, should occupy so much of her time. But the hatred and jealousy of Heloise grew day by day and absorbed her very being. Heloise was never long absent from her mind. There was a natural repulsion—almost a necessity to destroy her. There was no peace while Heloise existed, no repose. Of all Noel's conduct—his visits with Neville, his very attitude while there—Carlotta was fully and minutely informed through her housekeeper Maud. Maud, once and for many years a snubbed, and miserable governess, had eagerly taken the post of housekeeper under a peeress. But she had nothing to do with jars and pickles, never hardly ever heard of butcher and baker. These were not her concerns. She was well educated, rather subtle, though suppressed; had some remains of beauty; was no bad foil to her mistress; and she was older. Carlotta had her constantly about her. Her business was undefined, for she had nothing to do with the toilette—in point of fact it consisted in ministering to the tyrannical caprices of her mistress. A mistress who in every other word sneered at her poverty, her age, her small pretensions to beauty; who flung the cruel usage of the world in her face as if it had been her desert, and occasioned by her fault. A mistress who trod upon her finer feelings day by day, and purposely with intent to wound, and with delight in torturing. O, but the gold! The salary was high. Poor wretch! Through Maud and the servants at Louis's place Carlotta knew everything—had almost hourly information. The sting of it was that Heloise made no effort; was even unconscious, it seemed, of Noel's admiration. Now Carlotta had had to make an unusual effort to secure him for a brief and passing hour. But he followed Heloise of his own accord. Carlotta was un-bearable at these times. Maud had serious thoughts of leaving her, even despite the loss of the salary, but for Victor. Victor was in London, expected daily at Carlotta's—to see his aunt for the first time. So she endured

it, finding no peace but in the oblivion of
sleep. Carlotta conjured up in her mind a
vision of Heloise as described to her, sitting
surrounded with Georgiana, Neville, and Noel
in those happy winter evenings. She sneered
and laughed at this poor and silly amusement.
She expressed and she felt the uttermost contempt for Neville and his science, for Georgie
and her theories. But in her heart of hearts
there was a bitter yet unconscious envy of
these men and women who could thus find
happiness and content in pursuits not only
legitimate but laudable, and even beneficial to
the world. Another reproach to her. She
hated them; she almost cried for the power to
ruin them all. The thought of them embittered
the glittering joys of her life. She could not
enjoy Rome without destroying Carthage. She
listened eagerly to the whispers of society, to
catch the slightest hint, the merest indication
that the tide of scandal was setting on Heloise.
In vain ; she met instead inquiries after Noel.
People asked what had become of him—why
was he no more seen with Carlotta? Per-

haps there was the faintest sound of an ill-concealed delight in these whispers and mur-murs that passed round from house to house and circle to circle, the faintest suspicion of a pleasure in the fading charms of Carlotta, who had so long preyed upon society, to the detriment, and the envy, and jealousy of the marriageable female portion. Maud caught at this sound, and magnified it. It was a chance to repay upon Carlotta some of the bitterness she had herself suffered. She dwelt upon it, delicately and by hints, but with suf-ficient distinctness to bring it home to Car-lotta's mind; and then sat down, and sated herself with the sight of the raging tigress tearing her heart to pieces with temper and chafing violence. It was in this mood that Louis found her. She burst upon him, called him a coward, a poltroon, a fool, to let Noel flirt thus with his wife, and remain looking on unconcerned, unavenged. Louis stared: to do him this much of justice, he had never conceived the possibility of Heloise permitting any such proceedings. Unconsciously, his faith in her was great; so that although he had sneered at Georgie and Neville and Noel, he had never for a moment thought of anything of the kind. Therefore he stared, and finally burst into laughter. Carlotta ground her teeth.

'Let us consider,' said Louis, utterly unmoved. 'If what you say is true, then we may find a method to be rid of this idiot.'

Then Carlotta hissed into his ear a plan that she had formed, and elaborated to seeming perfection. Let Noel have every opportunity; encourage him, throw Heloise upon him, lead them to compromise themselves, then expose them. Louis could thus obtain a divorce.

The sister persuaded the husband to connive at the projected disgrace of his wife. Louis listened, and smiled assent.

CHAPTER XIV.

Horton Knoyle, Esq., the banker, even now did not wish his nephews Victor and Francis to be introduced to their aunt. But when young men grow to the age of five-and-twenty and four-and-twenty they are not to be kept in complete seclusion any longer. It is a necessity for them to enter into society. Now when once Victor and Francis entered into society, society would very naturally soon begin to talk and make remarks if they were not on speaking terms with their aunt. When Victor and Francis therefore left the clergyman's house in Sussex and came to London, they had instructions from their uncle and guardian to call upon Carlotta. These instructions were given with much anxiety and with great reluctance; but still they were issued. Both the brothers were eager to see their aunt.

The very fact that they had been carefully hidden from her view all these years served to stimulate their curiosity, and they had heard rumours even in that quiet Sussex house which added a zest and edge to their curiosity. Victor especially, bolder and more energetic, penetrating more into company, had heard tales of her and her marvellous beauty which filled him with a restless desire to see her. She was no humdrum aunt of daily life. In point of fact she did not seem like an aunt or relation at all to them. She did not seem to belong to Horton Knoyle. It was almost like being introduced to a famous singer or actress.

Carlotta had looked forward to this ultimate meeting with Horton's probable, and indeed announced, heirs with no little interest. In the abstract she hated them. In the person she thought that most probably they would be boorish and a fearful bore. But they had about them the all-important fact of Horton's enormous wealth. She had no children. There it was, Horton was no longer

young. He was hard upon sixty. She more
than suspected that he suffered from heart-
disease. He was impenetrable—not a hint
ever escaped him; his physician was a man
of strict integrity, and politely warded off
the soft insinuating questions even of his
patient's wife, as no doubt he had been instructed to do. Not that Horton was an invalid; but still he was occasionally visited by
a physician. That fact could not be concealed
from Carlotta. His declining physical vigour
was evident enough. All this had caused her
many anxious hours of thought. The money!
It was not that she was in any way dependent
upon the continuance of his life for the supply
of her daily necessities. Horton had made a
large and liberal settlement upon her at the
time of her marriage. But accustomed for so
long a time to unlimited resources, the income
arising from the sum which was absolutely
hers appeared absurdly small. It barely supplied her dress. Not even the almost uncontrolled supply of cash which Horton allowed
her could meet her extravagant expenditure.

Unknown to him she had contracted large and heavy debts. She was, it is true, by law entitled to a third of his personal property at his decease. But Carlotta, though she had no conscience, had a brain. It never occurred to her to stay her course, or to seek to reingratiate herself with him. But she inwardly recognised the reality that a breach had long existed between her and Horton. She knew that he was aware of her improper intimacy with Louis. He was a man of steel. He would not show it, or own it in any way; but she felt that he would never forgive it. Full well she knew that her chance of receiving any of his property apart from her own jointure was entirely lost and gone. If he had made a will she had no doubt whatever that her name did not appear in it. Victor and Francis would probably take it all. Therefore, and to some extent not unnaturally, she hated them, and at the same time dreaded the news of Horton's decease. But for that reason, because she hated and detested them, all the more she desired to see and know them. It was her instinct to fondle and make much of those whom she wished to destroy.

The brothers were in ecstasies with their welcome, Victor especially. He talked of her incessantly. He compared her to all the famous and glorious women history has told of or poets invented. He positively raved of her. It was not wonderful that he did so. He was young; he had been much secluded; he was of a particularly ardent temperament; and he was inordinately vain. His youth and inexperience allowed him to be dazzled; his ardent temper led him to form daring hopes; his vanity made him an easy victim. It was so irresistible to have a woman so much superior in age, so resplendently beautiful, so admired and fêted, devote so much of her attention to him. He was her slave, her bondsman. He would have done her bidding let it be what it might. His whole mind and soul was full of her, and her only. She became a passion, and held him. She overthrew all the ordinary landmarks of his mind and conscience, making him insensible to the

calls of honour or of natural affection. Victor
was entranced. And Francis? Francis said
nothing. He was usually silent, undemon-
strative. After he had seen her, he seemed
to retire more and more into himself; to
brood over his own existence. Gradually a
crevice opened between the two brothers,
till now so warmly affectionate. Victor, finding no response to his enthusiasm, chafed and
sulked, and drew off, and spent his time either
with Carlotta or at least away from Francis.
Francis did not attempt to detain him. He
grew of a sickly hue—pale and sallow. The
truth was simple enough. If Carlotta had
excited the wildest imaginings in the mind of
the fiery Victor, she had absolutely overwhelmed the weak and feeble younger brother.
She in all her glorious beauty had entered
into his soul, and driven out his own identity.
He brooded upon her night and day; he kept
her photograph constantly before him, and
hung over it. Slowly but surely a smouldering fire of jealousy grew up between these
two. Francis could not talk as Victor could.

He was shy, retiring; nothing could draw him out. Victor pressed forward, said his say, laughed, and used the whole faculties that he possessed. Thus it was that in all company he received twice the attention of the other. Till now Francis was rather glad of this. He rejoiced in his brother's social success, especially as it left him alone and undisturbed. But now he regretted his own shy manners, which he could not shake off, and envied Victor's readiness, till in the end it grew to be a bitter jealousy. Carlotta saw all this. It was part of her plan. Thoroughly she understood the old maxim, ' Divide and rule.' She paid far more attention to Victor; this maddened poor Francis. But secretly she every now and then encouraged him, and at the same time she contrived to rouse a suspicion in Victor's mind that Francis received favours unknown to him. This to Victor was wormwood. It was worse than open preference. He boiled and raged inwardly. He cursed his brother; not in his hearing, but when alone—a much worse sign.

All this time there crept about Carlotta's mansion a pale and trembling miserable wretch. It was Maud. A bitter, bitter jealousy arose in her mind. She had feared this, foreseen it. It fascinated her to watch Victor with Carlotta. The iron went right into her heart, and festered there. She saw his bright and happy face beaming with joy if Carlotta favoured him. She saw his frowning look, his fiery glance, if Francis or any one else received a smile. She saw his eager desire, his ardent worship. Her very blood turned cold, and she shivered, as she watched. And she knew that Carlotta was playing with him—playing as a cat would with a mouse. Can anything be imagined more wretched, more miserable, than the position of this woman—guilty herself, conscience stricken, at least to some extent, and watching the partner of her guilty joy, the man for whom she had risked all, thus throwing his very soul at the scornful feet of her tyrannous mistress? It was, indeed, a cruel punishment for her. But it did not chastise her, it did not reduce her to remorse and contrition; on the contrary, it roused up a fierce and burning desire, not only for revenge upon Carlotta, but to plunge headlong into irretrievable ruin and disgrace with *him*—a disgrace and a ruin from which there should be no withdrawal, but in which lowest infamy he should be entirely hers. Before condemning her utterly, listen to what Pierce at Avonbourne, the gentle and the good, has to say upon these things. Victor had no eye for Maud. He never saw her. Her poor and watery sunset paled and faded away before the brilliance of this starlit night, which 'walked in beauty,' and shone with unapproachable glory. Maud longed to destroy her, to trample her in the dust. With a bursting heart she searched her breast, ransacked all the old memories to discover if there was no secret with which she could cast the proud idol as with a lever from its pedestal. The idea of writing to Horton and revealing the fact of her mistress's familiarity with Louis, of which she was perfectly well aware, and pos-

sessed indisputable proofs of, often occurred
to her, but was as often put on one side by
the reflection that, in all probability—in fact,
she felt no doubt—Horton knew of it already.
But she watched and wished; ready to pounce
upon Carlotta, and tear her to pieces with
unsparing hatred.

This playing with the brothers came as
a sort of interlude to Carlotta. It soothed
her mind a little. She did not forget Heloise;
but it distracted her attention for a while. It
sustained her over-weening vanity to find that
her charms were still irresistible. She boasted
of this aloud to Maud in her dressing-room.
She laved her magnificent bust, and called
to Maud to come and look upon it; and
taunted her with the want of such splendid
curves. She triumphed in her intense vitality.
'I am forty,' she said; 'only five years younger
than *you;* and look at me! You are faded;
your complexion is turning yellow and bilious.
I am white, firm, smooth, full. Ah, the men
cannot resist me. I am a goddess!' And she
laughed in Maud's face, and showed her white

teeth. It was insufferable; it drove the wretched creature frantic. She could have stabbed her upon the spot. But this is the peculiarity of these women: they hate each other to the death; they spit venom over each other, and torture each other with horrible glee. But they lay no physical hands upon the detested object. Such things only occur in novels; in real life women never stab or murder. They feel it; but they never do it. They fight with sharper weapons than steel, with weapons which pierce to the very soul, and sting it to torture and misery. Thus Maud·stood outwardly patient and calm, listening apparently unmoved, yet ready at the slightest opportunity to dig the dagger of moral and social vengeance into that shapely and voluptuous form. Playing with these boys was an interlude in the great drama to Carlotta. It refreshed her, revived and strengthened her. But the catlike instinct within her drove her too far. She excited them too much. Thus thrilled to the very inmost core with envy and jealousy, a collision was inevitable. It came at last, simply enough. It was a dusky evening; they were both at Carlotta's. Victor was in the drawing-room with her. Francis had somehow wandered into the conservatory, where he sat alone, brooding, brooding, brooding. Presently Carlotta left the drawing-room. Victor chafed at her absence—grew impatient; at last determined to seek her. At that very moment Maud was watching to get an interview with him. She waylaid him as he approached the conservatory; but seeing Francis, stepped aside. Victor heard the rustle of her dress, but did not see her. He thought it was Carlotta—Carlotta, who had been alone in the dusky conservatory with Francis. In an instant the long-suppressed rage burst forth. He called his brother a fool, and worse. Francis rose to his feet, pale as death, but without a tremble in his limbs. He faced his brother, but said nothing. In an ungovernable rage, Victor, construing this silence into assent that Carlotta had been there, struck him full in the chest. Francis staggered, but with a cry returned, and feebly hit out. Then the devil rose in Victor, as he felt the weak blow, and with one strong fierce thrust of his muscular arm he drove Francis headlong down and through the frail support of the plants, crashing into the hollow space beneath. His head struck the brick pavement, and he laid still and silent. Victor turned on his heel with a curse, and left the place. Then Maud stole out from her hiding-spot, and helped up the fallen man. He was insensible; but her eau de Cologne brought him to in time. He groaned once, and only once. Then he besought her to help him to a cab. She got him out somehow by the garden entrance, and into a hansom.

Maud returned musing to the house, to find Victor bending over Carlotta, as if nothing had happened. She went upstairs, and taking out her desk wrote to Horton an account of what had occurred, of the terrible fascination Carlotta exercised, of the fight, and Victor's utter abandonment to the wiles of his idol. At first she tried to disguise her handwriting, but she found all effort needless. Her hand shook till the scrawl was barely legible. She easily insured its safe postage. She must get Victor separated from Carlotta, or her heart would burst.

There is a tragic and ancient story, a legend of the far-off and distant past, which tells how, of two brothers sacrificing to God, one struck his fellow and killed him, and thus introduced death into the world. It was one of Louis's wicked sneering remarks, that he never could understand how one man could kill another over a mere difference in religion, over a sacrifice. Had there been a woman in dispute between them, he could have more easily credited the death of Abel at Cain's hands.

Not that Francis died, or was even seriously hurt. In a sense, it was not he who was slain; it was Victor who morally died.

CHAPTER XV.

IT was the more dangerous for Noel, because he saw Heloise grow more and more beautiful every day. He had not at the first seen her in the full splendour of her loveliness. She was pale, weak, an invalid, shorn of half her beauty; yet even then she had fastened his attention. But now, day by day, as she grew better and stronger, and the hue of health returned to her cheek, fresh loveliness suffused her whole being, as the glow of the dawn lights up the grey sky of morning. If she had touched his heart before, how much more dangerous was it not now! At first he questioned himself—doubted, argued with himself; but that was a process that could not long continue with Noel. He simply ignored all questions and doubts and per-plexities, and went on visiting and seeing her week after week, without once asking himself to what all this must tend. He said nothing, did nothing to hint in the faintest manner at his love; but it was absolutely necessary to him to see her. It grew upon him; the days when he was away from her were inexpressibly long and weary. Till now he had looked upon Georgie as rather a bore—a very estimable person, but too much occupied with abstract ideas to afford amusement or company. Now she became invested with an attraction not her own ; the light of Heloise lingered on her. Noel cultivated her friendship; he even entered so far as in him lay into her theories. He did not do this from any deep design; he was incapable of forming a deliberate plan to deceive. It was the unconscious outcome of his rising passion.

Georgie was constantly with Heloise; it was natural to pay attention to her. On her part Georgie was delighted to find a new proselyte. She worked hard at Noel; she exhibited all her stores of argument and thought in the endeavour to enlist another champion of women's right. In the heat of this pursuit she never noticed that Noel's gaze was for ever upon Heloise; she did not observe his abstraction, his abrupt answers and disconnected questions; nor did she notice that she was herself giving him an opportunity of almost constantly seeing Heloise. Thus unconsciously Georgie acted as a screen to allow these two to meet; and thus she also afforded facilities for scandal to fix upon Heloise's name. How bitterly she would have blamed herself—how decidedly she would have stayed the progress of things, if only she had seen this! But she was blinded. So it was that for weeks and weeks Noel sat with Heloise, and drank-in her increasing beauty day by day, and watched her being in all its outward manifestations. All this while there was no thought of Louis in his mind. As he had to Heloise, so Louis had struck himself out of the sight of others. The scar upon Heloise's lip had driven him from his rightful position: Noel never thought of him. This was absolutely true; Louis never entered into his thoughts, yet the consciousness that Heloise was married did. But the man she was tied to was an abstract idea, no personal reality.

Louis meantime was never seen. He had completely abandoned his mansion. They never heard his name; they never saw him, or had any conception of his whereabouts. No one recollected when last he had been at home, no one had heard for where he had departed; they were left entirely to themselves. Gradually, too, it seemed as if all old acquaintances dropped off one by one. In the morning Heloise remembered that friends used to call incessantly; even during her illness the carriages were constantly at the door. These had dwindled in number, till now the roll of wheels was never heard, the bell was never rung; the house was left alone, solitary. Heloise recognised this with a sigh of relief. While she had been ill she could avoid seeing people under that pretext. She had prolonged it as far as decency would allow. Then she had seen several. They did

not make too curious inquiries, but her sensitive organisation felt that they were criti-
cising the scar upon her lip; so that it was
a relief to see no one, and she did not remark
upon it.   It was what she preferred; and
in a little time all thought or notice of the
change passed away from her.   A new enter-
tainment had opened for her.   She was tired
of reading; the fanciful heroes and heroines
had lost their interest from reiteration.   She
had begun to cast about for a new mode of
passing the time.

Hitherto Noel had sat silent at their
evening meetings—silent and watching; but
by slow degrees the sense of restraint wore off,
and he spoke.   Heloise learnt from Georgie
of his wondrous travels, and she pressed upon
him to relate them for her gratification.
Noel, who could never be persuaded to write
a book, hung back and hesitated; but she
drew him on—she was really curious.   Then
he began.   At first it was a mere bald narrative of journeys, how one day he was here,
and another there; but the questions of the

listeners drew from him minute particulars: thus he was led on to details. In the end, a glowing graphic narrative flowed from his lips; such a tale of adventure and danger as it had fallen to the lot of few to dare, and to return to tell. Heloise became spell-bound. Her gaze fastened upon this man, her eyes never moved from his face; but her soul, her thought was far away, following the ideal or abstract Noel through these perils of the forest, the desert, and the deep. That abstract wanderer became endowed and sur-rounded with all the halo of her own imagi-nations, till at last she woke up and saw her hero before her in tangible reality. Then Heloise grew meditative and thoughtful; from her mind, too, Louis had utterly de-parted — it was open, free, unoccupied. Therein from that hour there grew up and increased the image of another. The thought of love never occurred to her. At that time, perhaps, love had not been born in her heart. But she dwelt upon him; he was not as other men. There was much in his complete contrast to herself. He was so grandly, so heroically bold—so godlike in disregard, in command almost, of danger; she was so sensitive, so shrinking, and timorous. Never before had she met a man of this class; they had all been commonplace — carpet-knights. This man had fought with Nature, had met her in the innumerable fearful shapes she had assumed, like the magicians of old, and had overcome her. He had encountered her in the form of the desert, the blinding sand, the fierce heat, the burning thirst; he had met her in the forest, with its fever, its beasts and serpents; he had met her upon the vast and illimitable ocean, face to face with her raging storms and thunder; he had met her in a still worse shape—in the shape of human beings dead to all human feelings, brutes of the wild and desolate places. Couching his lance, he had rushed at them all, and over-thrown all, and conquered all. In his own person he had accomplished those very deeds which others only read of and wondered at. There was a fascination about the man—the fascination of ten thousand dangers. Multitudes go to see the man who exposes himself to danger. How many hundreds of thousands hung upon the motions of Blondin on the high rope! With what eager anxiety and interest men rush to the shore to watch a shipwreck, or tear through the streets to the site of a fire! But this man Noel, danger, death, disease — all horror and fear sat upon his brow, and played with him, and he with them, as the snake-charmer toys with the fatal serpents. He stood apart—a being by himself; and she mused upon him, thought of him, and wondered at him, till there arose in her gentle and affectionate breast an almost motherly yearning and tender care for him— a sympathy deep down in the very core of her being. She could have stroked him smoothly with her hand, she could have arranged his pillow for him, and watched him slumber, holding her breath lest he should awaken. Deeper still arose a reverence, an almost fearful reverence of him. He was of another order—very Fate and Destiny themselves had marked him. She never thought of Louis; but subtle analysts of the human heart and brain may perhaps claim that there was something in all this of the revulsion, the recoil from Louis's utter lack of those qualities she now felt the influence of. He was artificial to the very centre, a scoffer, carefully avoiding all personal risk, scoffing at the brave as fools. There is no need to dilate on what Louis was—*we* have seen him. She herself never recognised this; daily her mind and soul centred themselves more and more upon Noel. The manliness of his bearing fixed itself before her mental eye, and she saw him always. There came a time, too, when she remembered the years at Avonbourne, and the teaching she had imbibed there at the hand of Pierce—the teaching which drew its deepest lessons from the works of nature; from the sky, the sea, the hills, and the trees. She remembered her visions upon the hill-side, lying on the soft and velvet turf, dreamily watching the slowly-driving clouds, or the shadows over the golden fields of wheat. Soft memories of these dreams and aspirations—aspirations without a name — came back upon her. Verily it seemed as if this man Noel was the very hero, the very human impersonation of these idealities, these voiceless hopes and imaginings. They had come to her at last in shape and form and tangible reality. Thus Noel came to be surrounded with an atmosphere of all things beautiful and desirable. Gradually and imperceptibly she grew to dwell upon his coming and his going—to watch and wait for his arrival, to sigh at his departure, and to restlessly long for the intervening time to pass. She entered upon a new existence; the monotony of her life passed away; the days were dull and long no more; the weariness and ennui faded; the slow step, the lack of energy, the languidness, were overcome. Her step once more was quick and free, her eyes sparkled and danced as they had done in the olden time at happy Avonbourne. The restlessness, the vivacity returned: she sang as she walked about. The physicians saw this, and announced that she was well; Georgie saw it and rejoiced, without the slightest suspicion of the cause; Noel saw it, and was overcome. This was still more dangerous for him. He had pictured her as quiet even to a fault; now he saw her in all the glory of her natural spirits and buoyancy. The infection of her joy caught him, and he put away all thoughts and perplexities to revel in the pleasant present. Still no thought of Louis.

There was a magic about Heloise now that she had not possessed at Avonbourne in her earlier time. She was as young as ever—not only in years, but in manner and ways. But there was the additional charm now of a sense of depth that had not previously existed. She was almost too light and gleesome at Avonbourne—too childish, too much like the foam, and the foam only. Now there was a solidity, a depth behind the gladsome ring of her voice and the sparkle of her eyes, which impressed those who saw her with a more lasting memory. Her form too had altered and improved. She had been a little too slight, too fragile. She was slender still; but the arms were firmer, rounder, the neck and bust fuller. She had all the youth of the child, with the charm of the full-grown woman. Once—and once only—a thought crossed Georgie's mind, as she looked at her, of how dangerously lovely she was. Women, even when the dearest of friends, are not apt to dwell on the beauty of another. The thought passed away as quickly as it came, but the memory of it recurred to her in after times.

Thus, without a thought of evil, the germ of unutterable love sprang up in Heloise's heart.

CHAPTER XVI.

It was a difficult task that Georgie had now before her. Though they had lived so long on familiar terms, though they had travelled together, and had conversed upon almost every possible topic, yet she hesitated and faltered when the pressure of fast-flying time brought on the necessity of discussing their marriage. Had all gone on as it had begun —had no difficulty arisen in her mind—there would have been no reluctance on her part. Previously she had not avoided the subject, but spoken of it freely and without reserve. But now that her mind had been shaken and her confidence upset by the miserable consequences of marriage as she had witnessed them, she experienced the utmost reluctance to speak upon the subject, and most of all to Neville. He noticed this, but he attributed it to the natural modesty of her sex, and it caused him no alarm. He did not press her for the cause, or question her as to her meaning. This put her in still greater difficulties. She had hoped that he would press and question her, that he would open the subject: instead of which, time went on, and Neville, perfectly contented, said not a word, while poor Georgie, ever growing more doubtful, knew not what to do, and was afraid to address herself to him lest he should doubt her love and reproach her with deceiving him. At last, however, she made up her mind, and with many an' inward tremble launched out boldly into the inevitable argument which she knew must follow. She began about Heloise; she pictured poor Heloise's unhappy alliance in strong and vivid colours, and painted Louis in his true light. The inference was plain, that marriage was a dangerous enterprise—a voyage against which there was no insurance. But still Neville would not take her meaning. All he said was that Georgie need not fear—all this did not apply in any way to *them*. They had known each other for a length of time; they understood each other's habits and grooves of thought; they were not as others; they had an evidently happy future. So that Georgie was compelled to state in plain and unmistakable words her full meaning, conscious all the time that Neville was listening, not only with amazement, but too probably with a growing anger and distrust. What she meant was this. Personally she feared the risk of marriage. She knew and appreciated the worth of Neville—she never for a moment supposed him capable even under provocation of the atrocious conduct of Louis; still she had a dread of the unknown. Apart from her own concerns also there arose the question of the right and wrong of marriage. Was it as it at present stood an institution truly and in all completeness in accordance with those laws divine which Heaven had impressed upon human nature, in the same way as laws of motion, for instance, had been affixed to material nature or matter? She confessed that she

had many and great doubts on this point. As
a feeble instrument, as an earnest seeker after
truth, was it her duty thus to assist in her
own person at the perpetuation of marriage in
the present condition of that institution ?   In
plain words, she did not want to marry under
the existing laws of matrimony.   Neville listened to this confession in the most utter
silence and surprise.   He was taken completely off his guard; he had not the remotest
conception that anything of this kind had
been working in her mind.   The first impulse
was one of anger and distrust, just as she had
feared.   Why had she so long concealed this
from him?   But as she proceeded, and as he
marked her evident confusion and the difficulty under which she laboured in explaining
herself, this feeling wore away, and in all love
and tenderness he set earnestly to work to
combat her decision.   It was unfair, he said,
to judge of marriage by the unfortunate example of Heloise and Louis.   One example
did not prove a case.   If she argued from the
evil result in this instance that all men were

liable to stray and to err as Louis had done, he might as easily argue that all women were evil and wicked and unfaithful because Horton Knoyle's wife had done as she had. Georgie in an instant snatched at this remark. It proved her very own conclusions; for, said she, she admitted that the woman was as often at fault as the man, and she could not guarantee that she should never give him provocation. This was all nonsense, cried Neville, really cross for the moment; it was impossible that *his* Georgie, his own true Georgie, could ever be as Carlotta was. That woman was an exception, a rare occurrence. It was an insult to him even to suppose that he should ever even ask any one at all like her to marry him. If she (Georgie) had ever exhibited the faintest trace of a disposition resembling Carlotta's he would never have continued so long in her society. Then Georgie, beaten and driven back in the personal argument, but unconvinced, widened the scope of the discussion by bringing in the general aspect of the question. To look at it in a philosophical and distinct light, was it a natural contract? The man by the very words of the marriage-service was to be considered as a being immensely superior to the woman—a creature so much grander and nobler that the woman was made to swear that she would obey him. Now one of the first principles of that small but heroic band of persons of which she had the honour of being a member, however unworthy, was that the woman was really equal to the man. How could she then swear in all honour to 'obey' —that was to surrender up her very soul, to give up the right of private judgment? That very right of private judgment for which the martyrs of the Protestant cause had so cheerfully died, as the first and most fundamental of the relations between the creature and the Creator. If, then, she as a Protestant did not surrender her judgment to the priest, the holy Church, the representative of Heaven, how could she surrender it to a man, a person of whom she believed herself to be the natural equal?

Neville did not attempt to argue this point

with her. He knew that it would arouse the dearest prejudices of her sect. He contented himself with saying that the phrase 'obey' need not in their case at least be taken in so full and expansive a sense. She must know full well that he had no desire to tyrannise over her, to control her either morally, mentally, or physically. Had he ever shown any disposition to do so? Had he not ever, on the contrary, rather bent his own inclination to favour her views? But if the experience she had had of him was not sufficient, he would go still further. At least she knew she might rely upon his honour. He would give her his most solemn word of honour—he would take an oath if she pleased—that he would in no way attempt to control or interfere with her in the slightest degree. That would surely satisfy her and meet her objection. No, she did not mean what she had said in that way. She did not suppose that he would ever take advantage of the power which the law would give him—a power, by the bye, which no oath or promise could deprive him of. The law

did not recognise illegal contracts. But he
really quite misunderstood her. He must remember that all men were not Nevilles ; all
men had not his intellect, his calmness, his
generous forbearance. She stood forward as
the representative of woman in general, she
did not demand her own rights; it was in the
interest of her whole sex that she hesitated to
enter into matrimony. What then, asked
Neville, did she mean? What was the ultimate meaning of all this? Were they never
to marry—were they ever to remain apart,
mere friends, acquaintances, fellow-students,
no more? Georgie was unprepared here. She
had no ready answer—her heart beat too fast.
This came home to her. She could not rise
completely superior to her own feelings ; yet
she managed to say that such must be the
case, at least till some alteration took place in
the marriage-laws. Then Neville threw his
arms round her and held her close, and gazed
earnestly into her eyes—eyes that faltered and
turned away from him. Did she really mean
this seriously, or was she only trying him ?

Surely she never could mean it? Surely his Georgie loved him? Her head drooped on his shoulder, and her eyes filled with tears. Love him—love him? He knew that her whole heart was his. Then why not let love assert its supremacy and overcome these mere shadowy objections, these mere fancies of the mind. To her—so highly intellectual—after all, these acts of parliament, these institutions as they were called, could be really of no consequence; she could see beyond and through them. Let love assert itself and conquer all things. For the moment he almost convinced her. She wavered and gave way. He pressed a warm and lingering kiss upon her lips, his embrace tightened. He pursued his advantage. He could feel her heart beating and throbbing tumultuously. But suddenly she burst away from him, and stood up to her full height in all the majestic beauty of her stature and her statuesque shape. The mind within, whether mistaken or not, exercised its dominance over the heart and the feelings. The mind conquered. She hesitated no more.

She declared her purpose firmly, decidedly: she would never, never marry under the present laws. She loved him—she confessed it freely, openly. Never should she love any other—never forget his memory, or what he had been to her. Always he would be her dearest friend, her chosen companion; always he would be her leader, her adviser. But never, never would she reduce herself to the level of a slave chained for ever. Then she turned and fled, not trusting herself to say more.

Neville was left alone. He was literally overwhelmed, it came so unexpectedly upon him. But yesterday happy in the anticipation of the rapidly approaching union, and now in a moment the ground was cut away from beneath his feet. He felt giddy, his head seemed stunned. He hardly knew what he did, nor could he fully realise the position. It was days before he recovered himself, and once more, with renewed love and affection, set himself to overcome her rash resolution. He did not attempt to argue, he even totally ignored the subject; but he showed his love more plainly than before. They had been so long living on familiar terms and in such constant intercourse, that to a certain extent those little attentions and courtesies which are the language of love had been neglected. Neville renewed them. He watched her every motion, he anticipated her very thought. His hand lingered in hers; there was an increased warmth in his glance, a tender intonation in his voice. The intense affection of the man spoke out from his entire being. This was very trying to Georgie. At first she attempted to ignore it, to pass it off; but the endeavour was useless. She could not; her woman's heart clung to him, her being thrilled at his touch, her heart hung upon his words. Gradually she melted. Nothing was said about marriage, but the reserve which Georgie had begun to maintain melted away. She basked in the sunshine of his love; she gave herself up to the intoxicating delight. She told herself that this was allowable at least; in this she did not desert her post and her

mission. She did not recognise that in this
very abandonment of herself to him she was
even then surrendering her private judgment ;
that at that moment she 'obeyed' him in the
true spiritual sense. Her soul answered to
his, and moved now this, now that way, as his
inclined ; her mind was absorbed in his mind.
This was obedience in its most absolute and
highest excellence. In the silence of the
night, alone in her bed, Georgie, unconsciously
to herself almost, was engaged in working out
the problem how to reconcile this complete
and utter devotion to Neville with the usages
and the requirements of modern society.
Was there no means, no way of enjoying the
intense and heavenly happiness without surrendering her post and mission, and yet at the
same time satisfying those requirements of
morality and decorum which society properly
and rightly demanded should be observed ?
She did not put the question before her in so
many words, but it was constantly present in
her mind. The instinct of love was certainly
implanted in the human creature by its Crea-

tor ; it was born with it as much as the instinct of eating and drinking. It was therefore as lawful to indulge in the one as in the other. More than that, if society by a traditional usage—by the laws of marriage in fact—prevented a rational creature from following that instinct, then society constituted itself a law-giver, and took upon itself to oppose nature and Heaven. In other words, if she was prevented from marrying Neville by the irrational and unrighteous nature of this contract, if she was compelled to accept an illogical contract or to abstain, it was evident that society was not only wrong but guilty. Heaven gave her a mind, and in giving her that mind commanded her to use it. By using that mind she discovered that marriage as at present contracted was irrational and led to the worst consequences. But Heaven had also given her a heart and bade her love, and it was her right to indulge that love as much as it was her right to think and act for herself. Therefore those who opposed the free exercise of both these endowments, of the

mind and the heart, must be opposing the will
of Heaven.   Was there no way of reconciling
the laws of nature with the laws of society?
This was her problem night and day.

There came a time when an idea dawned
upon Georgie which seemed to promise to go
fairly towards solving the difficult and com-
plex question.   Her modesty recoiled from
it at first; but she conquered her modesty,
at least this species of modesty, in the same
way as she had conquered the allurements
of her feelings.   Slowly and by degrees she
thought it out and planned it all.   Then
with this came a certain complacency, a glow
of satisfaction, that she had been chosen to
inaugurate a new era, to set an example for
all time to follow.   Out of this feeling grew
up a resolution to carry out her purpose, let
the world say what it might, let whatever
difficulties occur.   Her love and her enthusiasm in her cause she felt sure would carry
her triumphantly through.   With one bold
step she should free her sex from the trammels
which bound them.   She should be the Ma-

homet, the prophet of a new social dispensation. She would sacrifice herself unhesitatingly, freely, to procure this great and inestimable advantage to her kind. Upheld by the strength of her faith and of her enthusiasm, she would face the burning fires of scandal, and finally conquer the dark armies of prejudice.

CHAPTER XVII.

PERHAPS of all the trash that was ever written or printed nothing equals the abominable bosh which issues day by day from the French press as fiction. This is speaking of course in the aggregate. French novels there may be unoffending at least; but the mass are infected with a corruption unsurpassed in its foulness. Yet out of all this vast heap of loathsome scurrility there may be gleaned at least one exceedingly bright and resplendent jewel. Among the odd and fantastic creations of the prolific pen of Alexandre Dumas there exist three chapters worthy to be enshrined in the very cathedral of literature. And of all other books these chapters are to be found in *Monte Christo*—that most improbable work. Yet there they are—precious gems set in lead and hidden beneath loads of verbiage, unnoticed by the careless, scarcely alluded to or ever thought of in the works of other authors. These chapters detail the life and labours of the Abbé in the prison on the French island. The sailor who is confined in the deep dungeons of that structure for some alleged political offence passes months in a state of mind which changes from a maddening rage and impotent restlessness to a condition of mental stupor, utterly overcome and conquered by the oppressive loneliness and the war of his own passions. It is then that, sitting in silence and perfect repose in his cell, he becomes gradually conscious of a slight knocking sound, a dull and muffled thumping apparently proceeding from a depth beneath his bed. By slow degrees this noise becomes more and more loud; but it invariably ceases a few minutes before the gaoler visits him with food; hence he naturally concludes that it is some prisoner endeavouring to escape. Impressed with this idea he waits till the sound recommences, and then stamps with his foot; instantly the noise ceases. In this way he establishes a means of communication with the other, and at length by the removal of a stone, a narrow tunnel is exposed, some twenty feet in length, running through the solid wall of the prison fortress. From this tunnel emerges the person of a prisoner — the Abbé. These two become friends, and the sailor is introduced to the Abbé's labours. This man has been confined there for many years. In vain he waits for release, and offers millions to be permitted to reënter life. This offer of millions leads the authorities to the belief that he is mad. Even the sailor, struck as he is with the Abbé's ingenuity, is a little staggered with the other's persistent claim to be the discoverer of enormous fortunes. However, he listens to the story. The Abbé was secretary to the Cardinal Spada, who, himself poor, was the descendant of a cardinal *tempore* Cæsar Borgia, who possessed fabulous wealth, and was in fact poisoned for that wealth by the famous son of Pope Alexander VI. But after his death not a ducat of this enormous treasure could be found—it had vanished, and Borgia was disappointed. A tradition survived that it had been hidden on some desolate and uninhabited spot from a dread of this very assassination. The Abbé, secretary to the modern cardinal, exercises his ingenuity in endeavouring to discover these lost millions, but fails entirely, till the Cardinal dying bequeaths to him his books and a few hundred scudi. After destroying the private papers of the deceased, the Abbé sits in the study mournfully recollecting his virtues and friendship till the increasing darkness causes him to light a lamp. For this purpose he snatches up a piece of parchment lying as a marker in a breviary that had belonged to the assassinated cardinal three centuries previous. As the parchment shrivels in the flame he observes written characters stand out, revealed by the heat from the secret ink in which they were originally inscribed. He blows it out, but on inspection only sufficient remains to show that it was a memorandum of the ancient cardinal of the spot where he had buried his treasure. All the directions and indications of the spot are burnt, to his intense chagrin. But the Abbé with ceaseless patience, and with extraordinary ingenuity, restores word by word, and letter by letter, the missing guides, and at last produces a perfect copy of the original paper, with full directions as to the place of burial of the treasures. These directions he is about to follow, when he is arrested for political purposes and cast into prison. There he remains for years making applications to various parties to release him, and offering millions of money to the prison authorities to connive at his escape. They laugh him to scorn as mad. During all the time that he does not abandon hopes of release from without the Abbé is engaged on the most ingenious works. He constructs a sun-dial, by means of which and a ray of sunlight that enters the window, he is enabled to measure the flight of time. He makes ink with the lampblack from his lamp and the oil which feeds it. His paper he supplies by tearing a linen shirt into narrow strips. On this he composes a history of Italy, writing the more important passages in blood drawn from his own arm. His pen is made of a piece of fish-bone, taken from the fish supplied as food. He makes a geometrical calculation of the thickness and direction of the prison walls, and having laid down the direction a subterranean tunnel must pursue to enable him to escape, he sets to work to drill it through the solid wall. His food is supplied in an earthenware dish; this he breaks, till it is brought in a species of iron pan with a handle. This handle he uses as a chisel, and with it by degrees works out stones and mortar, till at last, after years of labour, he arrives under the sailor's cell, only to find that by an error in his calculation he has deviated from the proper course, and is no nearer escape, while his increasing age and feebleness prevent him from further effort. But even then he submits with unfailing patience. The contrast between the restless sailor and the calm, patient, persevering, ingenious, and almost divine Abbé, is striking in the extreme merely as a dramatic fiction.

These chapters ought to be printed in gold letters, and distributed by the societies in London which busy themselves with the moral education of the masses. They should be hung up in crimson and purple covers in the study of every man who claims the pre- rogative of thought. They should be printed at the end of the Apocrypha, as in themselves the finest record of human wisdom, worthy of admiration in all time to come. The man who could write them must have been, with all his faults, no common individual. The lessons they teach are simply sublime. The conquest of human patience, of human inge- nuity and ceaseless labour over matter, over all the obstacles that could be presented to it, was never so strikingly shown. Out from the very page starts up a voice crying, 'Go thou and do likewise. With such patience, such perseverance, such ceaseless labour and inge- nuity, there is nothing thou canst not do, nothing that need in any wise appal thee.'

This is the inestimable jewel in the toad's head of French filth.

It was with this 'eternal patience,' this endless ingenuity, and unfailing perseverance, that Horton Knoyle, the millionnaire, had built up his colossal fortune, bit by bit, and step by step. From the low position of the second son of a country gentleman, barely rich enough to give his eldest a profession, and only able to afford an education to the rest, Horton had risen by the sheer power of his own mind to be the companion of princes and the friend of kings. By tiny morsels at a time his mind of polished steel had bored its way clean through the thickest walls of society—to emerge in what? The story of the Abbé has its sad side too. He emerged in a dungeon. Horton emerged in— But we shall see.

It was part of Carlotta's plan to avoid alarming Heloise. If the slightest rumour reached her ears that people had begun to talk of Noel's visits, then her scheme was at an end. Heloise would take the alarm, and be upon her guard. Outwardly at least all would be well. In this plan Carlotta did not take into account the possible virtue of Noel. She set him down as the same as other men. Thoroughly she adhered to the belief that 'the thoughts of men's hearts are evil continuously.' It never occurred to her that possibly Noel might admire Heloise, even love to the verge of desperation, and yet stay at the verge, and go no further. She did not believe in human resistance to temptation. She had tempted too many, and watched them fall. Had she not, for a time at least, tempted this very man? Louis's absence from home was by collusion. He obeyed Carlotta's instructions to give the two every opportunity that could lead to crime. He went further than mere absence from home. He abstained from all society in town—saving Carlotta's, which he enjoyed by stealth—so that men said he was on the Continent. Then Carlotta spread one of those whispers which travel from house to house, unseen, yet rapid as the telegraph. There was a domestic difference—a slight, only a slight disagreement—between Louis and his wife. She wished to remain in total obscurity, unvisited, unnoticed for the time. It would be a kindness if people would not call, it was painful to her to meet others. Traced to Carlotta, to Heloise's own sister, the rumour was at once accredited, and acted upon; while at the same time it roused vague expectations of a possible *dénouement*, and prepared the ground for the ultimate disclosure for which Carlotta sighed. These steps succeeded to perfection. No one visited Heloise. Louis was supposed to be abroad. Noel went oftener and oftener. But after a time Carlotta grew dissatisfied with the progress of affairs. She could not wait. Her fiery vindictive temper, if it was not employed in scorching up others, must waste its energy in destroying herself. She ate her own heart, to use the old proverb; she gnawed at herself, and lived upon her own venom and hatred. This could not be borne. Noel made no progress, her spies informed her. He was no nearer now than he had been weeks previously, or even than when he began. He had not even opened his lips. Not a single assignation had taken place between him and Heloise; not a kiss had passed. The man was a milksop. A fierce contempt for him arose in her mind. She hated and despised him at the same moment. The lackadaisical idiot—the mere sentimental baby! But with this feeling there rose a parallel belief that through Noel's instrumentality she should never carry out her project of ruining Heloise; should never enjoy the spectacle of her disgrace and fall, to rise no more. Her hot blood surged within her and turned blacker and blacker with the violence of her spite. The very sense of impotence embittered it all. Never before had she failed; never before been baffled and made to feel her own powerlessness. Had she been Noel, how easily she could have subdued and enchained a female heart! With what ease she had conquered and enchained scores of proud men, the masters of the universe, the lords of creation, pah! the fools. But if man was a fool, woman was the merest plaything. Carlotta entertained the most ineffable contempt for her own sex.

Here was a man who could not subdue a child
—a mere child such as Heloise. The very incapacity he exhibited was maddening. The dulness of the dolt incensed her beyond all measure. Something else must be done. *She* must step in herself. Her hand must go to work. With ease she should conquer. If she were only a man, Heloise would fall within a month; and society should ring with her destruction. This creature longed to exchange her sex, that she might effect the ruin of her own flesh and blood. I call her 'creature;' the word 'woman' is disgraced in such a being. But this Carlotta lived, for I knew her.

In this frenzied mood of rage and impotent hatred there came a letter from Horton's solicitors. This was what she read, slowly, deliberately, as one spells out a death sentence:

'3 Gray's Inn, November 187—.

'My Lady,—It is with extreme regret that we are compelled to address you by the instructions of our much-respected client, your honoured husband. In so doing, we are discharging a duty as painful to us as the resolution taken by our client must have been to him. We are particularly requested to approach you with every mark of the most exalted esteem, and in any negotiations which may arise we are strictly instructed to extend the deepest consideration and the finest delicacy towards you. If in any particular we appear to deviate from these instructions, we beg you to attribute it to the lack of words in which to express our client's meaning in an entirely inoffensive manner: and not to any want of study on our part how to spare you the faintest annoyance.

'These were the words dictated to the active partner of our firm by Horton Knoyle, Esq., who telegraphed for his attendance in Paris: "You will endeavour to break this decision to Lady Knoyle in a form which shall spare her the slightest sensation of humiliation. She is aware that in the early years of my career, when fortune favoured me with the honour of her hand, I experienced the effect of a sustained and rooted passion for her equal in intensity to my admiration of her unsurpassed beauty. The memory of those times therefore increases the difficulty under which I labour in conveying the altered and estranged sentiments of which you will be the channel of communication. These are not hasty steps. The germ of the present movement on my part was sown many years ago by the thoughtless—I would not use a stronger expression—by the thoughtless conduct of Lady Knoyle; a conduct which exposed her to the comments and criticisms of society. These comments and criticisms pained me to the quick, accustomed as I had been the whole of my life to stand before the world unstained, unassailed. But this I passed over without remark; bearing my wound unseen, and unspoken of, hidden in my own heart. Since then there has been growing in my mind an increasing suspicion, warranted by facts that have come to my knowledge, that Lady Knoyle has overstepped the boundaries of mere flirtation, and has indulged in improper familiarities with Lord Fontenoy. My open use of that gentleman's name—a use which, if I am mistaken, may subject me to the severest punishment—proves beyond doubt or cavil that I am in possession of credible information, and that I do not act without warrant. Even this, however, I have overlooked and borne with; anxious that the fame and honour of my name should remain pure and unsuspected of an interior corruption by the world, willing to bear my private disappointment with that great object. Therefore I have permitted this intercourse with Lord Fontenoy to exist for a lengthened period; until indeed at last I had grown to bear the daily mortification of my secret disgrace with some little patience, hoping in the end that the better nature of Lady Knoyle might triumph, and enable me to heartily forgive her. But of late an occurrence has transpired which only came to my ears through an accidental and anonymous channel, but which I have since fully verified; an occurrence which it is utterly impossible for me to ignore. Having no children myself, I had designed that wealth with which it has pleased Heaven to endow me to descend after my decease to the two sons of my lamented brother. Anxious that these young men should escape the taints of the world, and that the evil nature which is implanted in every one should in this case at least receive no encouragement to send forth noxious weeds, I placed them, and continued them under the care of a good and benevolent man, till a period arrived at which it was no longer possible to retain them in tutelage. During that time I had secluded them from the personal acquaintance of Lady Knoyle. But I need not dwell upon this painful subject. Suffice it to say that on coming of age these youths were by my orders instructed to call upon Lady Knoyle. What followed it is indeed distressing to me to relate to you. The two boys, fascinated with the mature charms of Lady Knoyle, grew jealous, their long friendship was broken, and the elder struck his brother senseless to the earth ; this demoniacal quarrel being fomented by the aunt, their natural adviser on the loss of their parents. On making strict inquiries I find that this horrible story is indeed true in every detail. I also find, to my extreme regret, that all the care I had taken in the education of these youths had not prevented the elder from forming a disgraceful *liaison*, and from various acts displaying a vicious temperament. The younger appears to have been entirely misled by his brother, and by— But I will add no further words upon this matter. After this conduct upon the part of Victor Knoyle it becomes, of course, impossible that he can in any way inherit any part of my fortune, or expect any further interest to be taken in his career by me. I feel it also my duty, as trustee for my brother, in the fear lest the possession of too ample means may encourage his propensity to vice, to take the 42,000*l.* to which he is entitled out of his control, and to pay him instead a life annuity of 300*l.*, which I am empowered to do by the will of my deceased brother. Francis will remain in my will. It now remains for me to deal with Lady Knoyle. This last and culminating indiscretion, to call it by no harsher words, exhibits her character in a light upon which a favourable construction cannot by any ingenuity be placed. The matter therefore does not admit of argument or of compromise; strict measures are the only ones I can adopt. The course which after serious consideration I have resolved to follow is this; and I must entreat you to particularly impress upon her the extreme desirability of her at once and without opposition submitting to my decision, since opposition can only lead to exposure, and *as an event is approaching* which will inevitably and inexorably condemn her. From my will the name of Carlotta Lady Knoyle is, of course, expunged. It will be necessary for me indeed to entirely rewrite my testamentary disposition, which I propose to do speedily with your assistance. The jointure of Lady Knoyle was 100,000*l*. This jointure she no doubt believes she possesses entirely free from any interference upon my behalf. And such indeed was my intention at the time when my infatuation of her beauty was at its height. But it so happened that at the very hour when the deeds were to be completed, your late respected partner was on his way to assist in the completion, fell a victim to an accident, and died ere he could reach me. Thus it was that the marriage took place without the formal completion of the document; and in one word, as you yourselves are perfectly well aware, Lady Knoyle is entirely dependent upon my bounty. While therefore I advise her to retire from society, and to consent to a judicial separation, I do so with full power on every hand to carry out my intention. I propose that she should retire to some spot on the Continent or in America; and for that object I will allow her an immediate sum of 1000*l*.. all her jewelry, and a further annuity of 1000*l*.; which will be ample for all the necessities of life. The loss of that social position which she has hitherto enjoyed will be her punishment for that wanton indiscretion which could not rest satisfied with these advantages. In the event of her refusing to accept these conditions, there remains but one alternative—a divorce, to which extremity I am resolved to proceed. You, gentlemen, are aware that I possess evidence sufficient for that purpose; and in that event I shall absolve myself of all responsibilities as to Lady Knoyle's future existence. These are my unalterable decisions, and I request that I may be spared the pain of needless pleading, to which I shall lend a deaf ear. You will oblige me by immediate attention to this business."

'Such, madam, were our client's instructions; and we are compelled to beg your early reply to our communication.

'We remain, very faithfully and obediently,

'Your humble servants,

' WILLIAMSON, VERNEY, & Co.

' Solicitors.'

This 'business'! Carlotta read the letter through from beginning to end, slowly, deliberately, weighing every word, while gradually a faint tint of a rosy colour appeared on her cheeks, and deepened till as she ended her whole countenance was in a scarlet glow, not the healthy red of exercise or heat, but the scarlet glow of inward fever. Her large dark eyes flashed with unutterable brilliance as the paper fell from her hand. But her lips did not tremble. She remained there for a second or two, and then extended her hand, which did not shake, and rang the bell. Maud came. Carlotta uttered but one word—

'Brandy!'

But in that one word, in that scarlet flush, in the fallen letter, Maud saw that her bolt had buried itself right to the head in Carlotta's breast.

CHAPTER XVIII.

CARLOTTA had for many years anticipated an open rupture between herself and Horton. In the beginning of their married life, when she first used her fatal powers of fascination, she had even then a premonitory sense of a quarrel to come. But in those days she did not fear it—she rather did her best to provoke it, secure in her beauty, safe that he would return again to her feet. But Horton said nothing; never even let it be seen that he noticed her proceedings. Then she grew still more reckless and indifferent to his feelings. Time went on, and Horton made no sign. Yet even in the height of the excitement into which she plunged, and which was her daily bread, there still lingered in her mind an indefinite dread of the finale which instinct as well as reason told her must eventually come. When Horton left her almost entirely to herself; when he was away for months and months, without a letter, and without a hint that he existed, she revelled wilder and wilder, and dipped deeper into the sea of dissipation. This creature had no conscience, but she had a mind, and she had a subtle and unerring instinct. She knew that Horton's nature, cold as polished steel, hard as polished steel, would never bend; but the fear was—would it break, and would the ruin fall on her? Of late the sense that this ultimate end could not be far off had driven her faster and faster on the road of reckless infamy. She grew careless of disguise—she resorted no longer to underhand processes by which to obtain a guilty liberty; she walked openly in evil, as we saw her stalking brazenly through the streets of London in the dress of a man. There was a feeling that her time was drawing near its close—that the license granted by the fiend was near its expiration. What, then, was the use of disguise—disguise which was certain to be penetrated? She would waste no time—she would do all the mischief she could whilst she had the power. Thus it was that she exerted herself to foment discord and hatred between the brothers. Thus it was, too, that her envy and bitterness against Heloise increased in violence. *She* would not fall; she would endure when disgrace and infamy covered her own name. Carlotta hated her for this. So that it was not with any great surprise that she received the letter from Horton's solicitors. This was the reason that she read it through with such calmness; there was actually a certain amount of pure curiosity to see what the blow would be like now it was about to fall. But the end of it all stunned her. She had never anticipated anything like this. No such conception of utter ruin had ever occurred to her. The utmost she had expected was a separation by mutual agreement, with a handsome income to spend on dissipation and pleasure as she chose. But this cold-blooded judgment, this sentence as of a judge upon his throne, threw her completely off her balance. Even her iron nerves, her grand physical organisation, shook and trembled. In that hour the foundation of her life was displaced more than it had been in the whole of her years ; and a crevice opened in the walls which never closed again. For days she remained in a state of stupor. She went through her toilette, through the usual daily affairs, apparently unconcerned, except that there was an absent expression in her eyes. She was in fact sleeping—sleeping as she walked about, and talked, and ate, and drank. Her panther-like, her wild-beast nature fled to slumber as its refuge and its medicine. Slumber alone could restore her vitality. And this species of somnambulance did restore her vitality. About the fourth day she arose in all her old *fierce* beauty, if such a phrase may be used. Even Maud was staggered. Carlotta reared her head, like some magnificent flower that had been bowed by the storm, but whose stem was not broken. She stood up as proud, as untamable, as vigorous as ever in body and in mind. The gloss on her hair was as lovely, the glow of her dark eyes as bright, the graceful sway of her motion as enchanting as ever it had been. Maud was dismayed, disconcerted. Was it possible ever to have revenge upon this strange and inexplicable being? Would nothing crush her? Maud began to feel something of that superstition which in the olden times led men to load their guns with silver bullets, in the belief that the evil one himself protected the bodies of certain tyrants from the effect of leaden balls.

Carlotta, recovered in body, bent her mind resolutely to meet the difficulties which beset her as firmly and with as little hesitation as Cæsar Borgia might have done. She would conquer yet: it might be that she would be revenged upon them yet. The first thing she did was to pen a short message to Williamson, Verney, & Co., acknowledging their letter, and saying that she would formally reply to it after a few days of consideration. The object here was to gain time. Her first impulse was to send for Louis, that they might consult together. But she reflected that Louis was utterly as selfish as herself, as unscrupulous, and as little to be depended upon. He might even desert her entirely now that she had fallen. *That* she was determined he should not do. He should share her fall, come what might; how to secure this? But first, could she by any possibility outwit Horton? Could she throw any obstacles in the way of his will—could she prevent by stubborn resistance the execution of his decrees? Carefully she re-read the letter, and considered it point by point. She knew Horton too well to attempt to move his heart by any personal appeal, the day for that was gone by. A hundred chances to one he would refuse to see her; if she gained access to him unawares he would move away. He was as cold, as hard as polished steel. It was impossible to bend him. The next question was: had he in any way deceived her in order to gain his end? Was there any statement in that letter not grounded on fact? She was constrained to admit that there was not. She felt positively certain that Horton even in the last agony of hatred could never utter a falsehood. He was truth, probity itself, even to a fault. It was his pride that through that very truthfulness he had invariably succeeded in everything he had undertaken. She felt no doubt whatever that his statements were absolutely accurate; she remembered the accident to the lawyer on his way to make the marriage settlement. But up till now, as she had always enjoyed the fullest control over the interest of this 100,000*l.*, she had rejoiced in the fancied security of its being entirely her own. Did Horton deceive her in this? She recollected that once when she had written a cheque for a heavy sum on this very account it was returned to her. The banker would cash nothing above the amount of the annual interest. It was clear then that she really had no control over the sum itself. Yes, without any doubt, what Horton had stated was positively correct. He could leave her utterly penniless. The 100,000*l.* was completely in his hands. She had not a penny to call her own. Granted all this, now what were his terms?—a miserable 1000*l.* per annum and residence abroad. This sum was not sufficient to keep her in the bare necessities of life. It meant total banishment from all those scenes of pleasure—all those displays in which the greater part of her life had been spent, and which had grown to be second nature to her. She would just as soon have divorce, and freedom to marry again, without a farthing of money from him. She felt confident in her own power to attract some fool to her side. But at the same time there rose in her breast a raging hatred of Horton. This monetary meanness excited her beyond all bounds. Till she began to realise what this 1000*l.* a year meant she had felt no temper so far as he was concerned. But to deprive her of the very spirit and soul of life, and cast her in this wretched way into the outer darkness of banishment, aroused the latent ire within her. She registered a fierce vow to have revenge for this; but she had control enough over herself even in that hour of mortification to throw aside her temper for the time, and to bend the whole force of her mind upon the question of ways and means, upon dealing with matters as they stood. It again occurred to her to face Horton; to defy him; to run the gauntlet of public exposure and of the inevitable inquiry. It would cost him more than it would her. On her side there would be an *éclat* about it; on his nothing but disgrace. For the moment she even thought of going upon the stage, sure of success in her splendid figure and fine voice, for no other purpose than the humiliation of Horton. But she abandoned this as inapplicable at present. The question remained: had she any chance of successfully contesting an action for divorce? Her memory, not her conscience, quickly replied that she had none whatever. She remembered too many open works of darkness to entertain the faintest hope from such a course. There was one other thing too which she hardly acknowledged to herself, but which through all this maze of thought was ever present to her mind, and influenced every idea. It was the sense that the time drew near when she would be a parent—and a parent of what? There was no hope. She could not fight—her steps were fettered on every side:

> ' Not only what we suffer, what we *do*
> Fetters our course of life upon its way.'

One only thing remained, and that was to drag with her as many to ruin as possible, and like Samson to involve her enemies in her own destruction. What was her best plan? how could she insure the infliction of the most pain upon them all? There was Heloise ; how cut her to the quick and cover her with shame? There was Horton ; how humiliate him, and expose his age to sneer and contempt? How at the same time secure to herself the greatest measure of security from poverty? After deliberate thought and anxious consideration, it seemed to her that she could best succeed in all these points through the agency of Louis. He should go with her; he should elope with her. That would at once fell Heloise to the ground with bitter shame and misery. More than that, it might even lead to Heloise's own disgrace. Wretched, humiliated, demoralised by this open desertion on Louis's part, Heloise might succumb to the temptations of Noel, and soil her own purity. Also, in all probability, Heloise's friends would insist upon her suing for divorce; after Louis was divorced, she, Carlotta, could marry him. With all her subtlety, Carlotta here made a mistake, or at least raised a nice point: Louis could not marry his deceased wife's sister legally; how then could he marry his wife's sister while his quondam wife was still living? But to set that on one side, as it did not occur to Carlotta at the time. For the present Louis could support her; his means were ample. She might move in very little less splendour and indulge in very little less extravagance than she had been accustomed to. On all these grounds Carlotta determined upon attaching herself to Louis. He should accompany her; he should be the partner of her fall. Once decided upon this course, the question next arose, how to secure his attendance? Should she send for him; show him Horton's letter; throw herself upon his breast; confess her dependence; and conjure him by the pledge of their guilty love soon to see the light to stand by, and to accompany her flight?

Carlotta actually sneered at herself as she drew this not unnatural picture in her own mind. She knew Louis better; she knew that the old cynic would turn from her the moment she displayed anything approaching to feeling. To secure him she must contrive to surround herself with the *éclat* and the subtle attraction of a splendid wickedness. She did not despair of playing the part to perfection. Her spirits began to rise again, now that it all resolved itself into the mere pleasure of deceiving a man. Her crest rose; her bosom heaved with a proud consciousness of power. This was her plan: first she would intoxicate him with the delight of her beauty; she would dress as she had never dressed before; she would please his eye, his taste; his connoisseurship should be bewildered with her supreme loveliness. Gradually she would confess to him that her love for him was greater than words could tell; playing upon his vanity till he lost his head. Then she would rouse his hatred of Heloise, and hold out to him the prospect of divorce from her. Since they could not induce her to commit herself he could commit himself, which would lead to the same desirable result. She would inflame him with a bitter hatred against Heloise, and hold out to his cynical and devilish temper the opportunity of heaping coals of fire on Horton's head. She would dazzle him too with her wealth; she would whisper to him that the 100,000*l.* of her jointure was entirely at her own disposal; he would readily believe her, remembering her enormous expenditure. She would display her jewels, her unsurpassed diamonds. These would allay any dread as to cash and annoyances which might arise in his mind. But above all she counted most on the intense though secret pleasure she knew he would feel in the sense of his own inordinate attractions. To elope with a peeress, the wife of a millionnaire, the guest of empresses and queens, the admired, the much talked of, the very centre of society! He to do this, the *éclat* would secure him safe—certain.

And she did this. Why dilate on that scene, that interview, in which Carlotta outplayed Cleopatra, and hoodwinked the sharp wits of a man trained in the blackleg diplomacy of the lowest saloons of Europe and America? Louis agreed; and gloried in the idea.

It was a strange and never-equalled elopement. Carlotta coolly took the tidal train for Dover and Paris, passing through the very city where her husband was staying, and from thence to Venice, where she awaited Louis. Lord Fontenoy, having first calmly settled his affairs, and drawn a heavy sum from his bankers, followed her in about three days as if it was the commonest thing in the world. How contrasted to the usual hurry, the wild passion, the confusion of an elopement! In fact, it was merely a permanent assignation on the other side of the Alps. Before leaving, this precious couple left a parting sting behind them, truly characteristic of their amiable disposition.

Carlotta wrote a note to Victor Knoyle, in which, with many expressions of endearment, she told him that out of her indiscreet attachment to him had arisen a coolness, and finally a disruption, between her and her husband. Thus her attachment for him had proved her ruin. On the other hand, his attachment for her had proved his; for his uncle had resolved to cut him out of his will, and had determined to reduce him to 300*l.* per annum. All this, she had no doubt, arose from the treachery of Francis. Thus she hoped to foment the quarrel between uncle, and nephew, and brothers; and to have at least one vassal at command. She conjured him not to believe in any scandalous stories that might be set afloat concerning her; she was going to a friend's in Italy, and she would write to his club and enable him to join her.

Louis on his part carefully composed the

following paragraph, which he sent to the
fashionable morning paper, and which duly
appeared, and was laid on every breakfast-
table in Belgravia and Mayfair:

'The most singular and exciting rumours
have been current during the last two or
three days concerning the destination of a
lady and gentleman who have lately left the
metropolis, *en route*, it is said, for the Continent. The lady, who is a peeress in her
own right, and the spouse of one of those
princes of specie who are the real rulers of
the world, has long been renowned for the
remarkable and fascinating beauty which has
proved irresistible in the saloons of society
for a lengthened period. Her beauty, her
caprice, her extravagant expenditure, have
centred an extraordinary amount of interest
in her proceedings. The gentleman, who is
a peer of the realm, and himself only recently
married, as it appears, to the sister of the lady
with whom he has now eloped, has also earned
no little reputation for the eccentric, and at
the same time cynical, composition of his

character. The most peculiar feature of this startling rumour is, that the elopement did not take place in concert, with the usual accompaniments of confusion, and under the cloud of night; but that each party quietly proceeded by different routes, and after an interval of some days, to the rendezvous, which is said to be some city in the north of Italy. This event, with the *exposé* which must eventually follow, promises to prove one of the most striking features of the season.'

Thus Louis secured the *éclat* of publicity.

CHAPTER XIX.

SEASON after season the walls of Burlington House are hung with the works of artists in all varieties of skill: innumerable landscapes, portraits, historical scenes—memory cannot recall the kaleidoscopical changes rung upon the colours of the palette. They rest for a time upon these walls, and then pass away as the gorgeous clouds of sunset, in gold and crimson and bronze, linger a while in the west and finally sink into the darkness. Yet in all these innumerable pictures there are no two exactly alike; no two in which the colours are the same, the conception identical, the combinations of light and shadow precisely similar. Each artist lends his own 'colour' to his work; and so infinite are the resources of the mind, so infinite the possibilities of the soul, that perfect similitude is never found.

Our feeble powers of reckoning cannot conceive the numbers of human creatures existing at this present moment upon the earth. Ehrenberg, the great microscopist, was accustomed to say that the remains of two millions of once living and breathing insects might be found in a single cubic inch, I think it was, of mountain limestone. Take this cubic inch of stone in the hand, and one has a tangible realisation of the idea of two millions; this tiny square piece of solid stone represents them; it is the tangible idea. But it is not possible to apply this process to the human inhabitants of the globe. They cannot be estimated in the concrete. All that we can say is that they number so many hundred millions; a million of them cannot be held in the palm of the hand. And of all these, as Xerxes said, not one shall be alive in a hundred years; what incalculable numbers then, looking back, have existed upon the earth since time began! Every one of these beings more or less felt the influence of love, and not two of them in a similar manner. Each and every one in the studio of the heart worked eagerly and enthusiastically at his painting, portraying an image called up by the instincts of his being. Yet no two of these pictures were alike.

Heloise's love for Noel was a love peculiar to her own nature. She had never loved Louis. A mere child, she had been interested in him, even dazzled by him, led onward too by the influence of Carlotta, whom she had not then learnt to distrust. When once her hand was given, then she never questioned, never analysed her feelings, but endeavoured, in so far as in her lay, to do and feel all that love could dictate towards Louis. So pure was her heart, so entirely unoccupied her imagination, that the thought of a lack of love never occurred to her. She had never known that emotion, and the want of it did not affect her. Thus it was that she did not recognise her sensations towards Noel as love. The idea of analysing them never struck her—she did not pause or think, but walked on her way as if through a garden of flowers, unconscious of the yawning precipice beneath her feet. Partly this was Pierce's fault. He had trained her to be too unsuspecting. He had not taught her enough of that worldly wisdom which is essential in these days even to the most innocent of doves. As she trusted him, so she trusted others. She had no suspicion, neither of them nor of herself. Therein lay one of her greatest charms. The ladies of our day are so knowing. They look you through and through, and appraise you at your value. They count the buttons on your waistcoat, and spy out if the watch-chain be aluminium or pure gold. They see a trap in all your doings, a pitfall in your words. They are constantly *looking behind* you, as a cat will behind a looking-glass, to see what reality lies at the back of the reflection. But Heloise accepted the reflection, the image that met her eye in all good faith. So too she accepted her own emotions as good, and did not question or analyse them. You see, practically she had had no mother; that parent had died in her earliest infancy. She had been left to herself and to Pierce. A mother would have inoculated her with an innate suspicion of the other sex. She would have been taught to ask herself what her feelings towards them were—to distinguish between the permissible and the non-permissible. Pierce had never thought of these things. Simple old man, such ideas had never occurred to him. He had trained Heloise up in all that was true and good and lovely in his mind. He had made her believe the true and the good; but he had not instructed her how to perceive the advance of evil. The mothers of our day do just the reverse; they instruct their daughters how to instantly detect the approach of the cloven foot, and therein consists the whole virtue they impart. Heloise asked herself no questions. Just as with Louis in the early days of their marriage she had revelled, absorbed in the beauty and pleasure and excitement of the theatre, oblivious of all else; so now she gave reins to the most exquisite pleasure of Noel's society, and never once said, 'Is this good? Is it right?' Do not judge her too harshly. Even now she was but a child, barely twenty in years; hardly seventeen in ideas, in knowledge of the world. Louis, remember, had not taught her any of this knowledge; he had only sneered at her lack of it. But she was married — a matron; she should have remembered that sacred tie. Heloise had not been taught, as the daughters of the day are taught, the supreme importance, the overwhelming sanctity of that contract. She had had practically no mother; no one to invest the ceremony of marriage with all its full mystery and title to reverence; no one to show her how to fold her hands, and bow the head, and kneel down and worship the idol. Her education had been lamentably neglected. We Protestants sneer at the Roman Catholics because they say that the simple word of the priest transforms the consecrated wafer into the body of the Lord. Yet our mothers most religiously impress upon their children's mind, training them up from the earliest infancy to the belief, that the breath of the priest saying the marriage words trans-

forms them into something essentially different—absolutely new—from what they were
before. By this magical mystical ceremony
they are born again—renovated—transformed
—utterly metamorphosed. They are no longer
what they were before. Their very inmost
being is changed. And so deeply is this creed
worn in and engraved into the faith of the
daughters, that the latter, reading these lines,
will no doubt exclaim that of course it *does*
alter them. Now, pray, in what way? Do
they not possess the same souls as before? or
does the miracle-working ceremony endow
them with a new soul? Have they not the
same hearts, the same organs, hands, feet,
features? In what then does the change consist? Purely mythical and imaginary. That
it is so, that it is purely imaginary, you may
learn from Heloise. She had never been
taught these curious lessons. She had not
the slightest idea that after marriage she was
supposed to be composed of entirely different
elements; not the faintest suspicion that she
was expected to be metamorphosed. The con-

sequence was that she did not in any way attempt to repel the impact of emotions pleasant to herself. Just as she would have welcomed them when living the old life at Avonbourne, so she welcomed them now, and rejoiced and was happy exceedingly. You see that no magical change, no wonderful mystical renovation and new birth had taken place in her. Noel was not long in perceiving the change that had come over the spirit of his reception. He was no longer merely *received*, he was *met*. He could not but mark the sparkle in her eye, the pressure of her hand, the slight flush upon her cheek, the flutter of her manner. And he gave himself up to these. He was a man of few companions.

His time had been spent in perpetual warfare, the warfare against the wilderness of the hunter and explorer. He had had no chance nor desire to make to himself a wide circle of acquaintances. He had a club, but rarely used it; therefore it was that, when in London, his time hung heavily upon him. He had no amusement here—he was out of place.

When he saw Heloise, and grew gradually enamoured of her, it followed that he devoted the whole of his time to her. There was nothing to call him away, nothing to distract his attention. It would have had no permanent result if there had been; but such things might have caused a delay. As it was, he gave himself up entirely to Heloise. He could not be always with her in person, but she was always with him: in the morning, in the day-time, in the silence of the night, she was ever at his side. The man loved with all the fierce tropical heat of his nature; the same savageness—if such a phrase may be used—which drove him on through untold dangers and difficulty, from one end to the other of Africa, now drove him headlong onward in this career of passion. A new world was opening to him. Till now the hemisphere in which he had moved had been one in which the greatest pleasure had been the exercise of the bodily powers—the glory and glow of labour—the wild delight of the chase —the stern resolution which overcame hunger and thirst, braving all in the pursuit of one object. The world of thought and feeling—perhaps more particularly the latter — had been a closed book to him. At two-and-thirty he was a mere boy, a youth, in these matters. He had never loved before—he had never even flirted. This was wonderful indeed in this age of drawing-room passion, of carpet adoration. The reason of it existed in the immense physical development of the man. He found it impossible to stay in-doors. The air, the sunlight, even the bitter frost, were a necessity to him; he revelled in it, he bared his chest to it, his mighty muscles rushed to meet it. The vigour of the man forbade his pursuit of the ordinary amusements of budding manhood; which amuse-ments are these: to rise at eleven for twelve; to languidly breakfast at noon; to dawdle away the morning (!); to ride in the Park at five; eight, dine : the chief business of the day between seven and eight, and at all times, to follow wherever petticoats do show.

To Noel such a life was simply impossible.

He did not despise it; in point of fact, he never thought about it. He broke away clear at once, and never returned. Thus it was that he, strong man as he was, was nearly as foolish as Heloise in these matters. It never occurred to him in what light his constant visits and his evident devotion to Heloise might be seen by society, for the very plain reason that he hardly understood what 'society' meant. So without check, under the unconscious shelter of Georgiana's friendship, these two pursued their way, getting hourly more and more entangled in the inextricable web which men call love. Heloise was so very, very happy; everything seemed so delicious just at that time—the mere fact of existence was an inexpressible pleasure; she said so to Georgie. Profound and philosophical Georgie said that this feeling arose from her state of convalescence. In good truth, it was the dawning of a new moral and spiritual life, not the renewal of the physical and tangible. Once more, as she had done in the olden time at Avonbourne—only so much more intensely now—Heloise saw beauty in everything. The very apples on the poor old costermonger's truck, as it was wheeled along before the door in the street, had a glory and a beauty about them. The lovely tints of gold and red and green, so delicately intermingling, and lit up with the last departing rays of the autumn sun, shone out with a splendour in its ray equal to those luscious fruit-scenes which painters love to limn. The sunlight of her love lit up everything upon which it fell with hues and tints borrowed from her own soul. She moved in a dream—a dream that ever grew more absorbing, that abstracted her day by day more and more from the outward and visible world, till she dwelt in the circle of her own consciousness, utterly unaffected by the passing of time;—a dream from which the rude hands of fact and fate were on the very verge of awakening her.

Georgie had stayed the night. The morning paper had been placed on the table as usual, but no notice had been taken of it. The day passed away till in the afternoon Ne-

ville and Noel came in together. Neville
had seen the paragraph written by Louis;
he had heard too at his club the interpreta-
tion the world put on it, and a few inquiries
had elicited the fact that it was only too true.
He had immediately started to tell Georgie,
and had been met and joined by Noel. Neville said nothing to his brother; for in good
truth he, and he alone, half suspected his attachment to Heloise. At any other time
he would have endeavoured to turn Noel's
thoughts into another channel: but then he
was too occupied with Georgie—he half suspected it, but he did not plumb the depth.
But now at this crisis he held his tongue.
So they arrived at Heloise's—the one knowing too much, the other in ignorance, chatting
gaily.

Neville saw Georgie, and told her all.
Georgie broke it to Heloise. Just at that
very moment it so chanced that Noel in im-
patience had wandered from the reception-
room, and came upon them. Heloise's face—
pale as death, with an indescribable expres-

sion of mute and fearful questioning—struck a chill to his heart, and he paused at the door. In a moment the poor lip—the lip with the scar—began to tremble ; she tottered, and would have fallen had not Georgie caught her. 'O, take me to papa !' she cried, while a few tears forced themselves out and rolled down her cheek. Noel, in alarm, had sprung forward, and forgetting all in the excitement of the moment, he was about to take her in his embrace, when a shudder passed through her frame, she recoiled from him with horror in her face, and motioned him away. 'Leave us,' said Georgie, 'she is ill.' Much wondering, Noel went.

In that hour a sense of what she had been doing—not a full, but an awakening sense of her own guilt—had rushed upon Heloise's mind. Louis was guilty, but was she innocent? She remembered Noel, and her conscience smote her. The scales fell from her eyes, and she saw the incipient crime she had been committing. Thus it was that she shrank from Noel. On him too, when he learnt from Neville the truth, there fell a dark shadow, which dulled and deadened the indignation he would otherwise have felt against Louis. He marvelled at himself that he did not feel that indignation. He asked himself why; and his conscience taunted him with a secret joy that Louis had left her. A shadow of guilt fell upon him. He recognised his moral criminality : he started, and he recoiled, but it was for the moment only. Noel had never been accustomed to control his desires. His heart beat fast, and there was a giddiness in his head; but the strong purpose held good in his heart of hearts, and he knew it. Heloise must be his—as the very words of the Prayer-book put it—for better for worse, for richer for poorer.

CHAPTER XX.

Wiтн Pierce at Avonbourne it was summer the whole year round. Not the hot glaring summer of the middle of June; but the sunshine lingered with him in the drear days of November. It lingered with him for this reason: that he studied how to catch it, how to retain it. His winter-room faced the south, and opened upon his garden, the garden where the birds congregated; only this portion of it was enclosed with high walls, and these walls hidden with thickest hedges of cropped yew-trees. Thus it was that the reflection from the house of the rays of the sun whenever it shone, and the total exclusion of all winds and draughts, rendered this small square plot of ground, carefully laid down with thick tiles, warm even in winter. The great window let in every particle of

warmth and heat and light; but the projecting
balcony over it sheltered it from the driving
rain, and the double shutters and the thick
red curtains made it cozy, and impenetrable
to wind at night. In this tiled courtyard
Pierce could walk even when the cold winds
of November howled around the place. At
this window he could sit when the white November sun shone out for a few moments,
and enjoy its warmth, perceptible even then.
The beams of the sun lingered lovingly on
his grand old head, and cast its shadows on
the broad folio pages which were his delight
and study. I shall not stay to tell how Pierce
received Heloise when she came one day unexpectedly, just as Carlotta had done, rush-
ing to him in her misery and disgrace. His
darling—how could he receive her but in one
way? There was a time when even in his
breast there smouldered an anger and a
hatred, a just anger and a just hatred, against
the destroyer of her peace. There was an
involuntary clenching of the fingers, and the
teeth ground together. Why did he not la-

ment for Carlotta?—his own daughter, too, remember. He knew that she had inherited her mother's nature, the mother who had made his life a hell. He hesitated to pity her, for he was not certain that she had not been the ringleader. These were days of tumultuous passions—days of whirl and excitement, in which all normal conditions were reversed. But after a while the long peace of his mind came back again. He had been in a state of repose too many lengthy years for even this hurricane of infamy to do more than ruffle the surface, and then die away in waves following each other at longer and longer intervals—the ground-swell of the mind. Shall we own it?—the presence of Heloise, unhappy as she was, had something to do with it. *She* was with him again. There was a fond, an inexhaustible, though secret delight in that. Georgie had accompanied her, and stayed at Pierce's pressing request, not only out of her own desire to do so, but because she saw the imperative need that Heloise had then of feminine companionship. Even the affection of Pierce, deep as it was, could not altogether supply what Heloise wanted then. She begged Georgie to stay so piteously that the latter could not refuse. Hence she wrote to Neville, and asked him to come down to her own estate. That estate was not four miles from Avonbourne. When her father died, knowing that his eldest son's children were provided for—for that son had succeeded in his profession—and knowing, too, that the younger Horton was rich, beyond all need of help, he left his small property entirely to Georgiana. It was while visiting his aged parents that Horton Knoyle first saw Carlotta, and felt her fatal fascination. So it was that Knoylelands, as it was called, was but four miles from Avonbourne: and so Georgiana, anxious to have Neville near her—anxious, too, for her happiness—asked him to come down there while she stayed with Heloise. He could see her then easily. In the proximity of Knoylelands there existed the latent possibilities of infinite mischief; for when Georgie asked Neville there, she once again left out of sight the fact that Neville had a brother, and that that brother was Noel. But for the present there fell a lull upon them. Heloise, shaken to the core, sorely needed rest and quietness; and where could she get that rest and quietness so well as in the old, old house, with the familiar things around her, with Pierce ever near?— Pierce, to whom she clung as the frail creeper clings to the decaying tree, weak though its support may be. He was no true father, no loving parent, this Pierce, you will say, else he would have followed the guilty pair, and have drawn down vengeance upon them. Vengeance upon them—upon his own eldest daughter, upon the husband of his youngest —would you have had this? Or would you have had him go into the courts of law, and rake up the details of this miserable drama of evil passions for the delectation of all the prurient perusers of the papers, for the gratification of the million? Carlotta reckoned wrongly when she calculated that Pierce, with his detestation of evil, would at once take proceedings to procure a divorce. For Pierce, though he was a father, had in all these years of life learnt to be something a little more than man. Yes; let it stand as it is written. He had learnt to be something a little higher than man. Even to him this sudden revelation of wretchedness—it was as much to be considered wretchedness as detestable crime—had proved too great a strain at first. The old passions, the hot blood of youth, was not so completely dead but that there rose up a little of the rebellious spirit, rebelling against this terrible and never-to-be-recovered fall. But after a while it passed away, and the old peace came back upon him. Then there ensued a remorse, yes, an actual regret, that in his heart he had cursed them. He blamed himself : he saw that he too was guilty, in that he had given way to his anger and to his hatred. For Pierce had a belief, inconceivable to those who do not possess the metaphysical faculty, who are so absorbed by the outward things of this world, by what is written, and printed, and preached, that they cannot retire into themselves and calmly examine the truth. Not only inconceivable, but even heretic and wrong: a belief founded upon no creed or religion whatever, be it Pagan, Christian, or what not. As such it is difficult to convey it faithfully and to do him full justice. Words are so treacherous. All must have had experience of that. One writes a letter to a friend; there is a phrase in it of which one took no note at the time of penning it. Yet that phrase is caught up by the friend, and bitterly resented, and it is of no use to say that one did not mean it. So here, in endeavouring to write out this belief of Pierce's in words that shall convey offence to no one, it is difficult to do so without penning a phrase which some one or other will take offence at. Broadly, his faith was this: that there was no crime, no evil; that man could do no wickedness. In these times, as for many centuries, the very name of Epicurus is held synonymous with all the sensual indulgences which flesh is capable of. The term epicurean is one of reproach, of contempt; a term of luxurious and carnal meaning. Yet those who have read all that remains of that truly great and wise philosopher know full well that his system—the creed which he taught—was in no way conducive to such a belief. Only he, or some one unfortunately for him, summed up his theories in the short and epigrammatic sentence: that the chief good was pleasure. This therefore the evil-disposed seized upon and put into practice in their own corrupt and sensual manner. Whereas, declare Epicurus's own disciples, there never lived a man of purer and holier life; and what he intended to convey was that the chief good consisted in rational enjoyment, and principally in contemplation. But with all due deference to these same disciples, and to the glosses and commentaries of a later age, there is very sufficient reason to believe that Epicurus truly enough *did* mean that the chief good *was* pleasure, and pleasure of any and whatever description. But since he was a philosopher, and one of holy and pure life, and a man accustomed to metaphysical and

ethical discourse, it still remains to be discovered what was the true meaning he in his
own mind attached to this most unfortunate
phrase. Let us throw upon it the light of
modern science. Darwin informs us that the
chief aim of all plants and animals is to develop themselves, to so expand and increase
their size and extent as to reach to the fullest
organisation which nature has made them
capable of. And nature has so endowed
both the animal and the plant with sensations
contrived to act as incentives to thus expand
and develop themselves. Such are the sensations of eating and drinking—the plants
throw out their leaves and roots for that
very purpose—and these incentives consist of
a pleasure in performing those functions which
lead to expansion and development. From
this we see Epicurus's own true meaning.
The grand design of the Contriver of the
universe is the perfection of the whole of
His creation, and that perfection is reached
through the development of each individual.
That development is attained through the

incentives to pleasure, which its peculiar organs make it capable of procuring. It was in this sense that Epicurus said that the chief good was pleasure, since it led to the fulfilment of the design of the Deity.

Pierce applied this principle to his own daily life, and examined it as applied to the daily life of the multitudes around him, and to the whole social structure. He saw men drink and get drunk. This, society declares, is a crime. Our own sense of right and wrong declares that it is a crime. But what is drinking? It is one of those incentives to physical development; for without drinking no human being can survive. So too with all the physical passions. But murder, robbery, and so on? All these, argued Pierce, are committed through some belief on the part of the criminal that thereby he shall attain a certain pleasure, a certain better position. They are all striving for something better. The most coarse and brutal pleasure is in reality, when traced to its source, but a vague and rude aspiration towards a higher state. Of this higher state the man may have no conception; but he has the *instinct* to long for it. His action may destroy his chance of attaining it; yet that action was nevertheless though involuntarily done with that view. Now the great God of the universe is so wondrously, so inexplicably great and grand, that no human intellect can fathom His marvellous wisdom. It may, then, be just possible that since He has impressed these instincts upon man—this instinct to rise—that in His sight and before Him there may be no crime and no sin. Considered as man towards man, there is sin and crime; but in the celestial and before God there may be none whatever. For these evil things exist and go on day by day, notwithstanding that 'God so loved the world that He sent His only Son;' notwithstanding, too, that God is illimitable in power, and that He is directly opposed to evil. Plato had shown, thousands of years before, that this God could neither originate nor connive at evil. Hence it followed that in the abstract, and when entirely taken out of all human consideration, there can be no evil, and no crime, and no sin. These only exist in the relations between man and man ; there are none such in the sight of the great Designer. That such is the case there is the example of the Lord, who pardoned the very woman taken in adultery—in the very act. She had sinned towards man, but to Him she had not sinned. Let the mind for a moment raise itself above human considerations and social relations. Consider our position towards the lower animals. We slay them day by day ; and not only when absolute necessity drives us, but for pleasure. In the eye of the Maker of these creatures this too must be sin, if there were any. But let it not be thought that Pierce would therefore in any way connive at crime in man. Only he hesitated to judge. He withheld himself from that great and awful office. Even in his own house, in the secrecy of his own heart, he tried, in so far as in him lay, not to forgive those who had injured him, but to abstain from judging them, to abstain from saying in his soul, 'These have sinned.' This was Pierce's creed. This was what he had for years impressed upon himself. This, apart from the considerations of delicacy, was the reason why he did not follow or in any way attempt to chastise the guilty pair.

Safe at Avonbourne, Heloise heard nothing of the storm of surprise, of sneer, of witticism that passed over 'society' when the flight of Carlotta with Louis became generally known. It was a sensation such as could not die out in a day. Georgie rejoiced that she had come down into the country. She was so closely related to one of the actors in the drama, that she felt as if the arrows of criticism would whistle very near her.

END OF VOL. I.

LONDON:
ROBSON AND SONS, PRINTERS, PANCRAS ROAD, N.W.

www.ingramcontent.com/pod-product-compliance
Lightning Source LLC
Chambersburg PA
CBHW031028120726
47905CB00007B/2089